Leaving Stoneybrook

A PREQUEL

CRIPPLE CREEK SERIES

SARA R. TURNQUIST

MOUNTAIN
SUMMIT PRESS

If you would like to stay up-to-date on this and other series from Sara and receive a free ebook, sign up for her newsletter:

https://saraturnquist.com/list

For Kelly

CHAPTER 1

Intrigued

Was she completely out of her mind? Mary Foster stared at the pink satin ribbon. It stood out among the others—bright and brilliant. And nothing like her. Why did she blend in so easily? Was she not special enough to stand out? Not even a little?

She pulled her attention from such frivolous things and set her mind firmly on the task before her. This was not the time for her to take a flight of fancy. Ma had requested she gather a few things at the General Store and Pa would be by soon to take her home.

She sighed and moved past the small display table and the shiny strips of luxury. What did it matter? She was plain. A fancy ribbon would not change that. What did she think? That the pieces of pink poking out of her pale hair would make David Matthews notice her?

Her face heated at that thought. What a ninny indeed!

Directing her gaze to the barrels of fruit, she collected several apples as she thought over her list. These would conclude her shopping...at least for the day. Ma had struggled of late to do the simplest things. And so Mary found herself making these jaunts to town on a mission for Ma more often. But she didn't want to think on that either. Ma would be fine, wouldn't she?

"Mary?" The voice called from somewhere behind her. A voice Mary knew all too well—David's sister, Katherine.

Now? Must she face the Matthews siblings now? Her dress was certain to be in disarray with dirt smeared from the trip into town. Not to mention her hair, likely in shambles after being blown about by the wind. She was in no state for anyone to see her—least of all David.

Mary turned slowly, praying she was somehow mistaken.

Sure enough, there stood Katherine Matthews. But God had shown grace—David was nowhere to be seen.

Mary let out a breath. "Good to see you, Katie. What brings you to town?"

"Same as you, I suppose...picking up a few things."

Mary nodded. Of course. It wasn't unusual for Katie to make these trips for her mother as well. Though, not because Mrs. Matthews was ailing. The woman had likely never been sick a day in her life. An ache expanded in Mary's chest, but she fought it. Ma would be all right. The doctor had assured them all she needed was rest.

"Are you well?" Katie stepped closer, eyebrows gathered over concerned eyes.

What? Oh, she had become rather distracted with her wandering thoughts. "Yes, just...wondering."

A smile tugged at Katie's lips. "What about? Or should I say *who*?"

Mary's cheeks grew hot. What a thing for her friend to say! Did Katie know that Mary had a care for the younger woman's brother? Or for how long Mary had borne it? She couldn't. It wasn't possible.

"No," Mary said, then attempted to clear her throat...and

her thoughts. "I am just trying to remember what Ma asked me to get."

Katie peered into Mary's basket. "Apples, cinnamon, a swatch of fabric..." The girl's fingers roamed over the wares. "I daresay I wouldn't want to be eating at your house tonight."

Mary balked but then realized...Katie only teased her. "Pa requested a pie, and Ma has some mending to attend to."

Katie grinned. "Your ma is the best seamstress in the whole of Cripple Creek."

Mary's lips turned upward at the corners. "Yes. She has quite a talent." Yet another gift that had not passed on to Mary.

"I hope one day she'll make me something special—a bonnet maybe."

"Perhaps. I'm sure she would enjoy that if..." Mary stopped herself. Their challenges as a family were not so publicly known. Nor did her mother wish them to be.

"If what?" Katie looked at the shelf to her right and plucked out a jar filled with beets.

"Oh nothing." Mary shifted her regard opposite. Perhaps Katie would dismiss it as easily as Mary wished her to.

Katie sighed. "Well I, for one, am looking forward to warmer weather."

That was an understatement. Mary fairly iced over every time she stepped outside into these frigid temperatures. But this turn in the conversation was an opening. It gave Mary an opportunity to ask after Katie's family and take the focus off hers. "How are things at Stoneybrook?"

"Oh, the ranch is all well and good." Katie sounded bored. "Same old, same old."

"And..." Mary swallowed, fearful she shouldn't ask, but unable to stop herself. "...what of your brother?"

Katie's eyes glinted as she returned her gaze to Mary.

If Mary didn't know better, she would think Katie did know. Maybe she did. Would that be so bad?

"He is as difficult and boring as ever." Katie's gentle smirk betrayed that she wanted to say more. But what?

Mary shrugged and glanced in the direction of the counter, hoping she appeared every bit as uninterested as she wished she could be. As she did so, she spotted Reverend Jones's wife coming down the aisle just adjacent to their position. Oh dear, she had intended to avoid such a confrontation.

Grabbing for Katie's arm, Mary turned in the opposite direction. Perhaps escape was possible. But she wasn't quick enough.

"Mary Foster," Mrs. Jones called. "My dear child, however are you?"

Mary grimaced. She did not want to have this conversation. Least of all in front of someone as observant and intuitive as Katherine Matthews. Still, Mary had her manners. And she would not betray them, lest her parents get wind of it and give her a tongue lashing.

"Mrs. Jones," she said, turning back toward the older woman. "How lovely to see you."

"Of course," Mrs. Jones said as she stopped just short of Mary. "You are such a kind and thoughtful girl."

Mary forced a smile she didn't feel. If she could, she would duck under the ribbon table and remain there until everyone was gone. She hated these uncomfortable exchanges.

"I thank you." Mary fumbled with her basket as she ran a hand down her skirt. Though it was impossible to erase the wrinkles and dirt as easily as she'd like. "But I must be on my way. I have to get these things home before—"

"Yes, of course." The woman waved a hand. "But before you go, dear, tell me how your mother fares."

Katie peaked an eyebrow.

Few in town knew of her mother's condition. And those

few were the closest of family friends...and Reverend Jones, of course. And clearly his wife. Though, unlike Mrs. Jones, Ma's dearest friends knew better than to speak of something so private in a public place. There were too many ears. And even more judgments.

Mary cleared her throat. "She is well."

Mrs. Jones tsked, clicking her tongue against her teeth. "That is not what I am made to understand."

Mary felt Katie's gaze boring into her but forced her attention to stay on Mrs. Jones. Her hands felt as weak as if they had turned into porridge. Surely, she couldn't keep her grip on the basket's handle firm enough much longer. How could she escape this?

Putting forth her most sincere voice and expression, she said, "Ma has her days, but I tell you, she is well enough."

"Poor dear." Mrs. Jones went on as if Mary had not spoken. "I do pray for her recovery daily."

Mary wished she could roll her eyes, but she dare not. Was there no reprieve from this woman? She lifted a prayer that God would be gracious to her once more and open a way out.

"I thank you for your kindness," Mary said through clenched teeth, not able to hold on to her appearance of interest any longer.

"Well, we mustn't feel sorry for ourselves," Mrs. Jones admonished. "It's all in God's timing."

Mary held her breath to keep from pushing it out in her exasperation. "Of course." She doubted the woman cared as much for Ma's health as she did a piece of gossip.

"If you will excuse me, Mrs. Jones, I do need to get these things home." Without pausing, she whirled.

And ran directly into David Matthews.

David Otis Matthews didn't know what had hit him. Or who. But his hands came up to steady whomever had barreled into him. He opened his mouth to issue an admonishment when he found himself staring into brilliantly bright blue eyes. Familiar eyes. Whose?

He pulled back slightly, still ensuring that the smaller figure gained firm footing. The azure pools had widened and appeared every bit frightened by the clash of their bodies.

"Whoa," he said, keeping his voice gentler than he perhaps needed to. As he took in the features of her upturned face, he offered a smile. "You all right, Mary?"

She nodded, stepping away from him and looking at the floor as if something of great interest had happened upon her feet.

That gave him cause to worry. Had he injured her? He touched her arm. "Are you sure?"

"Yes." The word shot out, her voice wavering.

It did not ease his concern.

She peered up at him through long lashes and shook blonde hair that shimmered in the sunlight streaming from the nearby window. "That is, I am well. And you?"

Her features shifted and looked every bit aghast. Because she was embarrassed at bumping into someone? Or because she had run into *him*?

He settled his hands on his belt. "Never better."

Her face colored, and she looked down again.

What was this? Mary had always seemed friendly, even if a bit on the quiet side. But he had never known her to be downright shy.

Katie came alongside Mary and looped an arm around her friend's. "You just startled her is all." He couldn't help but notice that Katie's grin was a bit too wide and her manner a bit too outgoing.

Would he ever understand females?

He waved her off. "Nonsense." But as he looked at Mary, he had reason to doubt. She appeared rather rattled.

"Perhaps we should see you home." It was the right thing to offer, but he had to admit there was a selfishness in it. He wanted to ensure that she was truly unharmed. Maybe a ride to her folks' place would loosen her tongue.

"No!" The word shot out of her mouth. A bit too loudly. Her cheeks reddened all the more. She licked her lips and then said, "That is, I'm quite well. My father will be along to collect me shortly."

David nodded, not taking his eyes off Mary's delicate features. She always had a way about her that drove him to want to protect her, shield her even. What about her brought that out in him? Maybe her kind and gentle manner. Or perhaps her timid nature.

Either way, he often enjoyed her company and found himself wanting to linger when he was with her.

"I'll just be on my way, then." Mary pulled free of Katie's hold and tried to step around David.

He halted her with a hand on her arm.

She froze and looked from his hand to his face, then back again.

He released his grip. It had not been his intention to cause her discomfort. "I only thought to apologize." He shot her one of his most disarming grins. "I don't make a habit of bumping into people."

Her eyebrows rose. "I assure you, the fault is mine. I did not watch where I was going."

"All the same," he said before thinking, "I'd prefer you let Katie and I see to you until your pa comes."

That only made the color in her cheeks deepen. "Oh." She glanced toward the counter as if longing for escape. Was she not comfortable with him? How had he never noticed that before?

"Please," he said, lowering his voice, "Maybe we can find a bench. There is one just outside." He reached for her basket.

She allowed him to take it, only releasing her hold after a moment of hesitation.

Then he ushered her to Mr. Yerby, who greeted them and made short work of tallying her items. "Will that be all, Miss Foster?"

"Yes." Why did she sound so sheepish? Something was definitely off here.

"I'll put it on your pa's account."

"Thank you, sir."

Mary reached for the basket, but David beat her to it, lifting it with ease. Then with an arm outstretched in the direction of the door, he indicated that they go outside.

She gave a quick nod toward Mr. Yerby and didn't resist when Katie came alongside her once more. "Did you see the new gingham fabric? It would make a wonderful dress for the Valentine's Dance, don't you think?"

Leave it to Katie and her ability to chatter aimlessly... almost inanely. Though David had to admit, it seemed to put Mary more at ease.

They stepped into the brightness of the overhead sun. He was pleased to find the bench just beyond the General Store vacant. Without prompting, Katie all but dragged Mary to it, moving almost as if prodded.

Mary stole a couple of glances his way but appeared to at least try to attend to Katie's slew of questions.

"Do you plan to come to the dance?" Katie droned on as she settled on the bench, tugging Mary down with her. "It's only a month away. We should start planning our dresses."

"I don't know. It will depend on how—" Mary halted and swallowed. Was something more amiss? She was quite out of sorts today.

"Depends on what?" Katie did not seem the least bit sensitive to Mary's reticence.

"I just...need to ask my parents' thoughts on it."

Katie waved a hand. "Your ma always loves a good get-together."

Mary nodded and offered a small smile. "That she does."

It didn't deter David, for there was something wistful about her statement.

Maybe it was something personal...beyond the boundaries of friendship. Either way, he had not been invited into the conversation. So he allowed his attention to wander. Not that the ladies were apt to notice. Katie could make conversation with a fence post. And probably had.

Several of the townsfolk milled about, going this way and that. Nothing new there. Did anything exciting ever happen in this town? He could say that Bob Womack's discovery of gold several years' back would qualify. It had created quite a stir and drove some to scour their own land for any gold that may be hidden there. Not to mention the fortune hunters who flocked to the area. Cripple Creek had become home to quite the mining operation. David had no doubt this once sleepy town would become all the more interesting over the next several months.

David's attention landed on a well-dressed man walking by with Mr. Hammond. They were on the other side of the dirt road, but the pair came closer. David couldn't hide his curiosity. Nor did he try. The bank owner was known to have intriguing friends. And new individuals to the town were still a bit of an oddity.

The two men crossed the road and moved toward the General Store. Mr. Hammond's companion met David's gaze. Had he been staring? The man tipped his hat in David's direction.

Though a little put off that he'd been caught, David touched the brim of his hat in return.

The man seemed to think that an invitation and tugged at Mr. Hammond to alter course. What could the man want? Did he intend to work a swindle? Or did he wish to speak with the ladies? David wasn't too keen on that.

But as the men neared, Mr. Hammond called out. "How are you today, Mr. Matthews?"

It was still a strange thing for the townsfolk to address him so formally. When did he stop being just 'David'? Though this happened more often as he grew into a man.

David glanced at the ladies, who watched the exchange. Stepping in front of them, he hoped to block this stranger's path and even his view of them.

The men stopped just short of David's position.

"Mr. Green," Mr. Hammond said quite boldly. "I would like to introduce you to David Matthews. His father, Tom Matthews, owns Stoneybrook Ranch just south of town."

"Ah, yes," Mr. Green said as he extended his hand. "What a fine piece of property out there."

David looked at the proffered hand and hesitated before shaking it. Though he still questioned the man's intentions, it would be rude to outright refuse such niceties. And he did have some level of trust for Mr. Hammond.

As he shook Mr. Green's hand, he asked, "What can I do for you? You looking to buy land around these parts?"

"Goodness, no." The man half laughed.

David scowled. Was Cripple Creek not a decent enough place for him? Too rugged for an upstanding gentleman?

Mr. Green cleared his throat. "That is…I would be delighted to say I lived in such a glorious place, but I am unfortunately not in the market to relocate at this time."

Nice try. The man couldn't sidestep his insult that easily.

"What brings you to Cripple Creek then?" David was

already bored with the conversation and the airs the man put on.

"I work with the stagecoach." There was a lot of pride in Mr. Green's voice.

David would wager he ran the stagecoach operation in some respect.

Mr. Green continued, "You must have heard of the stage route that will come through this area. Even making a stop right here in Cripple Creek."

David nodded. He had heard that about town. But he was never one to count on something until it happened.

The man looked a bit flustered. Was David supposed to have reacted some other way? Was the man used to a different response? If so, David wasn't certain what that was.

"It will be a wonderful thing for your town. Bringing mail and packages much faster. And new folks to the area." Was he trying to sell David something? It mattered little to him.

David shrugged. "Maybe some that are looking to stay in our...*little* part of the world."

Mr. Hammond's face reddened—and not in the sweet way Mary's had. It did no favors for his affect. Clearly, he caught David's insult and wasn't pleased.

Mr. Green did not let David's slight slow him in the least. "I am looking for able-bodied men such as yourself to hire on as stage drivers."

"Why would I want to do that?" David was intrigued, but he refused to let on that he was. He wasn't sure he wanted anyone thinking—much less telling Pa—that he had any mind of a future other than the ranch. Even if that was a future he wasn't certain he wanted. And David was all too aware that Katie, though quiet, probably soaked in every word.

"Just think of the money you could make. But more than that, think of the adventure! You would be able to see many new places and meet all kinds of people. Tell me, have you always lived in Cripple Creek?"

David nodded.

"A young man like yourself should be free to see the world. There are so many opportunities for a strapping young man. Think of the possibilities! All you need is a little ambition and a willingness to do hard work, and you could really make something of yourself."

David opened his mouth to naysay Mr. Green, but the man's words gave him pause. Make something of himself? Could he see a future like that? A future where he could be his own man and not just Tom Matthew's son?

Looking at the boarded sidewalk beneath his feet, he tried to give off an air of disinterest, but he wasn't certain he couldn't hide his true feelings.

Katie was beside him in an instant. "He *will* make something of himself. And he has a future." Her rebuke of the man was sharp. More so than necessary. More than was polite.

Mr. Green and Mr. Hammond's eyes widened.

"Respectfully, sir," Katie added before shrinking back behind her brother.

"I see," Mr. Green said as he took out his handkerchief and dabbed at his brow. Was the man perspiring? It was far too cold for him to be overheated. "Well, Mr. Matthews, if you change your mind, Mr. Hammond knows where to find me."

The man smiled broadly at David and offered a quick nod in Katie's direction.

David wasn't sure he liked the way the man dismissed her, but she had been impertinent.

The two finely dressed men turned and moved off into the General Store.

Katie was at David's side in the next second. "Why did you let him go on like that? You're not interested in driving the stage are you?"

David sighed and tried to appear exasperated. "That's none of your concern."

Her eyes narrowed. "What would Pa think of that?"

He gave her a sharp look. "It's nothing to concern Pa with. Don't you go tellin' stories about such ridiculous things."

Katie crossed her arms, her stiff stance betraying her displeasure.

Mary rose and moved between the siblings. "I'm sure it's nothing, Katie." The young woman soothed with a tone that sounded more melody than words. "Your brother was just being kind."

Something about the way Mary defended him warmed his core. What would it be like to have someone on his side no matter what the world threw at him?

He shook his head. Not only was he unable to entertain marriage while he was still beholden to his father, but he was also in no position to court a woman either. Still, Mary would make some man a fine wife.

"I've got to check on the horse," he muttered before turning to Mary. "Are you sure you'll be fine until your pa gets here?"

She nodded. "Of course." Nervous laughter followed. What was that about? "I'll just sit with Katie for a bit."

He let one side of his mouth quirk upward. Then his gaze fell on Katie. "I'll be back in a few minutes to get you home."

Katie's features were still hard, but she nodded.

If only he could ensure she kept her mouth shut when they got home. If only.

CHAPTER 2

Troubled

Mary's father drove the horse homeward as she watched the mountains in the distance. So peaceful, so sure. Indeed they had stood the test of time, had they not? For her part, however, she could not feel more alienated from the steadiness of the landscape. She was flustered and worried—for her family, for her future. Her doubts and concerns, it seemed, were never-ending.

She avoided Pa's gaze—should he even happen to turn toward her—the entirety of the fairly short trip. He had been more stressed of late. Too stressed. It could not be good for his heart. That thought tore at Mary. But what could she say on that score? Nothing that would be of any benefit. Still, that didn't mean she didn't worry for him. Praying and fretting had been a much too frequent pastime of late.

Was anything in her life stable? Except this view greeting her every time she looked beyond herself and found the world a much bigger place. Too big for her small worries.

They neared the cabin Mary called home. What state would Ma be in today? It had been far too unpredictable these last weeks. Sucking in a breath and letting it out slowly, Mary reminded herself of the doctor's words. It would pass.

Pa pulled the reins to bring the horse to a stop. The cart gave a slight jerk in response. "Go see what you can do to help your ma."

Mary nodded, not trusting her voice to relay any level of confidence. Truth was, she was quite uneasy about what would greet them.

But she stilled her heart as her father assisted her down from the bench. Giving his arm a squeeze, she moved toward the front door. A glance back assured that Pa attended to the horse. Should she help him?

She shook her head. That would only wound his pride. So she braced herself and pressed onward into the cabin.

Pulling at her bonnet, she glanced about. Everything was still.

"Ma?" she called, struggling to contain her rising trepidation. Had something happened?

A clanging came from the back bedroom. Was that Ma? Was she in distress?

"Ma?" she repeated.

Still nothing.

Mary swallowed. She wanted to wait for her father. But Pa likely still worked to put the horse and cart away.

It was best she push down this uneasiness and face whatever was the matter with Ma.

Setting her bonnet on the small dining table, she moved farther into the dark recesses of the cabin. Dwindling sunlight did not help matters; the house had become darker and colder. Had Ma no thought to light a lantern at this hour or stoke the fire?

Mary glanced about. The curtains were drawn as well. Had Ma not bothered to open them today?

Perhaps Mary should not have gone to town with Pa. Ma may have needed her.

Mary steeled herself as she forced her feet to move on toward her parents' room. There was no way to know how Ma would be one day to the next. Letting her sleep had seemed a fine idea this morning.

Now in the doorway to the unlit bedroom, Mary strained to discern anything within.

"Ma?" she tried again.

A shuffling of the blankets betrayed that Ma was abed.

"Ma, are you well?"

Mary stepped into the room with shaky breaths. Should she open the window coverings? Or light a lantern?

A groan from amidst the bedclothes answered her and she moved to Ma's side.

"Ma," she pushed out the word with force. "Ma, are you well?"

The figure strained to sit up. "Mary?"

"Yes, Ma, it's me. Have you been in bed all day?"

Movement gave Mary reason to think that Ma looked about. "Have I?"

"Let's get you up." Was that wise? Or should she let Ma rest? Something within pressed her to urge Ma up and out of bed.

Reaching for the reclined figure, Mary quickly made contact with Ma's arm. Tugging at her, Mary helped her upright. She was sitting. That was something.

Mary's eyes slowly adjusted to the dim room. She watched as Ma rubbed at her face.

"What time is it?" Ma's voice was hoarse. "I'm so thirsty."

As she always was of late. The woman couldn't seem to get enough to drink when she was up and about. "It's nearly dinner time. Pa and I are back from town."

"Oh goodness me. Dinner." The older woman shifted,

swinging her legs over the side of the bed. Then she halted. And moaned.

"Are you unwell?" Mary asked again, as if she didn't know the answer.

"I'm fine, dear. Just a little...dizzy."

"Maybe you should lie back down." Mary did not wish to see her mother lose her balance and end up on the floor. Then where would they be?

"Nonsense. I'll be right as rain in a minute or two."

Mary knew that wasn't true. Still, she nodded and kept her hands on Ma's arm.

The front door opened and closed.

Mary shut her eyes. Pa. How would he react?

"Is that your father?" Ma's face turned toward Mary's.

"Yes, but you should stay here. I'll take care of supper."

Ma tried to stand despite Mary's best efforts to hold her back. The woman was stronger than Mary gave her credit for.

"Let me help you," Mary insisted.

Ma wobbled and clung to Mary, muttering, "These old legs."

Mary choked back her rising emotion. "I can help you to your chair."

"I need to get your father his breakfast. He has a big day."

Mary bit at her lip. "It's almost nightfall."

Ma gripped Mary's arm...painfully tight. How was she so strong?

"Have you eaten anything?" Maybe that was all this was—Ma needed something in her stomach. But Mary knew better. This was not just hunger.

"Don't mind me." Ma leaned into Mary as they moved toward the kitchen.

Pa had stopped in the middle of the great room, his down-turned mouth and strained features told that he was as perplexed as Mary had been. How much had he heard?

Mary redirected Ma toward the dinner table. "Let me get you some bread." She shot Pa a meaningful look. He didn't move, seemingly at a loss. If Pa hadn't a clue what to do, how was Mary to know?

She managed to settle her stumbling mother in a chair before moving into the kitchen and slicing bread. The loaf was hard; it was a few days' old. Holding back a sniffle, Mary set the few pieces she could reasonably salvage on a plate and brought it to her mother.

After ensuring Ma started eating, Mary stepped to Pa and, lowering her voice, said, "We need Doctor Shaffer. She is not right."

Pa frowned. Would he deny it again? How could he?

The silence between them stretched.

When he spoke, it was with hesitation. "Let's not bother the doctor again. You know how she gets if she doesn't eat."

"I do." Mary found a boldness she didn't know she had. "And it's not right. Something is very wrong."

Pa shook his head. "Nothing to it. We just need to keep a better eye on it. Make sure she eats regularly."

Mary deflated. How would they find the answer if Pa and Ma both refused to acknowledge how bad things had become? And what was the next stage of this ailment? Was it possible for Ma to get worse? With her unsteadiness and confusion on days like today, it was a wonder she didn't fall more. She could seriously injure herself.

Could Mary just stand by while her parents lived in denial? Yet defying Pa did not appeal either. But could Mary live with herself if this illness claimed her mother's life and she did nothing?

David directed the horse and cart onto the familiar dirt road to his parents' homestead. The simple entrance sign signifying that they had entered Stoneybrook Ranch swung in the breeze. His father would be finishing ranch chores with the hired hands soon. How glad David was for a reprieve today. Even if it had been to watch over his sister's trip to town.

The large cabin sat on the opposite side of the front pasture. Simple, yet more than adequate for those who called it home. His father had done well for himself. He had come out west with a handful of dollars and a dream...and made something of himself. Something more than he had been. Something beyond his meager opportunities in Tennessee.

Ma no doubt bustled about within the structure, preparing a dinner that would more than feed her brood. A smile teased David's mouth at the thought of her racing about the kitchen, set on meal preparation. Being in her presence was both peaceful and nerve-wracking. She had a drive, a desire to seize every single moment. How did anyone live with such passion?

As they neared, David considered the view of that which had been home for all his years. How many times had he found this vista to be a source of comfort? Of joy? But now his heart flooded with the reality that he felt constrained, limited. Even his chest tightened at the thought. And he ached for freedom from the suffocating press of his father's expectations. Would it ever end? Would he be able to break away and stand on his own?

It wasn't as if Pa needed him. How many trials had Pa overcome? Without David. And how many times had David seen him push through and do hard things to make this ranch work? He never leaned into David for any kind of help. No, Pa was a self-made man.

"What's the matter?" Katie's words cut through the cloud of David's thoughts.

"Nothing." He pressed his shoulders back. Would that alleviate the tension that had built up? He turned her question on her. "What's the matter with you?" The defensive ire that rose in him was wholly unnecessary. And he regretted the curt response as soon as it left his lips.

Katie jerked back.

Yes, he had blown it once again. What must she be thinking now?

"Don't snap. I just wondered why you slowed the horse so much." Her words were hard, but he knew better than to let it rile him. There was a tinge of hurt underneath the shield she held between them in that moment. All because of his thoughtless tone.

"Sorry." He looked off in the opposite direction. "I was just, ah, thinking."

"Oh?" Her voice lilted upward as if she suspected what had occupied his mind.

He hoped not. There was the real risk that Katie would blab about the stagecoach recruiter. How could he keep that from happening? That wasn't quite worked out yet.

"Yeah." He pushed the word out on a breath as he leaned forward, hoping an air of dismissiveness may help her lose interest.

It did not.

"What could be weighing on you?" The words were kind enough, but her tone betrayed a childish taunt.

"It's nothing. Just...thinking." He slapped the reins to encourage the horse to pick up step again.

It obeyed. The jerk of the cart caused Katie to grip the edge of the driver's bench. "David!"

Her admonishment did nothing to dissuade him from pressing the animal onward. So, she thought he was going too slow before, and now decided he pushed too hard? What pace would she like?

But he knew...it was his guilty conscience that had given rise to his resistance.

He did not respond, biting back any further words with teeth pressed into his lower lip. It didn't matter. Soon enough, he tugged the horse to slow once more and then halt.

Katie let out a long breath. "Was that really necessary?" Now the edge to her tone could not be explained by anything other than frustration.

He shrugged and hopped down, but he felt her intense glare as he came around to the back of the wagon. The sooner he unloaded these wares, the sooner he could have a minute to himself.

Still, she watched. The hairs on the back of his neck told him as much.

"You coming?" he called without looking in her direction. She huffed.

He knew he should come around and help her down. But he'd had enough for today. Katie had something in that head of hers, and from the way she glared at him earlier in town... the way she always glared at him when Mary Foster was nearby, he suspected it had to do with some idea of he and Mary. Katie hadn't had the easiest time making friends after Ellie Mae's accident. Mary had become a bit more than a good acquaintance to her. And it wasn't as if he didn't appreciate that she had someone.

But something about Mary set his heart to thumping. She was pretty for certain, with fair skin and petite features. It was more than that, though. How did she make his core warm with but one of her shy glances? He blew out pent up air. It was nothing. Even if it were something, he was not in any position to initiate a courting situation...with Mary or anyone, for that matter.

Did Katie have some grand idea that her brother and her

friend would be suited? He supposed that was only to be expected, but that didn't mean he had to cater to her whims.

Lifting the crate of produce, he then moved toward the porch.

Katie remained in the driver's box, arms crossed, lips pursed, the picture of adolescent irritation.

He didn't care. Let her sulk. Yet as he neared the front of the house, something tugged at him. Just because she was being petulant didn't mean he had to respond in kind. If he wanted everyone to treat him like the grown man he was, he needed to put aside childish attitudes and be the adult.

That made him pause. He didn't like it, but he knew it was the right thing.

He set the crate on the porch and strode back to Katie's side of the wagon. Then he lifted his hands.

She shot him a look that seethed.

"Come on, Katie, I'm sorry." He wanted to simmer, but that wouldn't help matters either. He forced his voice to remain even and calm. "Let me get you inside."

She jerked her regard opposite.

He set his hands to his belt. *Not this.*

How was he to overcome her need to save face?

He leaned closer, offering his most conciliatory expression as he softened his tone. "You know you're going to forgive me, so let's just get on with it."

Whether it was the gentling of his words or the pitiful nature of his plea that moved her, he did not know. Perhaps both had been necessary to appease her. Either way, she turned and loosed the tight clench of her crossed arms.

Considering him, it seemed she attempted to gauge his sincerity. Whatever she decided, she then reached for his shoulders and dropped down almost faster than he could catch her.

She giggled as she wrapped her arms about him and squeezed. "You know I can't stay mad at you."

He patted her hair and smiled to himself. Yes, he did know. Though the fact that she might well spill about their interaction with Mr. Green did not console him.

Yes, he knew her well.

She pulled back and rushed for the house.

He followed behind her, gathering the crate at the porch steps. Then he, too, stepped within.

The smell of Ma's beef roast greeted him as he closed the door with his foot. That was some consolation for the unevenness of the day. Ma didn't make it nearly often enough. Though, to be fair, he could eat it every day.

He glanced about the space. Sure enough, Ma rushed about the kitchen as Katie ruffled the fur of the ranch dog. How did she ever convince Pa to let her have that mutt in the house? Katie sure could work magic on him.

David stepped toward the table but found it had already been set for the meal.

"Where should I put this?" he called loud enough to get Ma's attention.

She turned, one had gripping the oven door. "Um…just there." Ma gestured to a space on the floor near the sink.

He obliged, taking in several deep breaths, savoring the wonderful aroma. If he were to ever leave—and that was a big if—he sure would miss Ma's food.

Who was he kidding? He would flat out miss Ma.

She opened the oven and reached in to pull out the pan near to overflowing with tender meat, potatoes, and carrots. Gritting her teeth, she struggled with the load.

He grabbed a towel and assisted. "Don't let that get away from you," he teased. "That would be a real tragedy."

Together, they settled the food on the stovetop.

Ma stood and pushed a hair from her face, smiling. "Not a chance. But thanks."

An overwhelming urge to embrace his mother filled

him. What was that about? It wasn't as if he had a real chance of getting out on his own. Not yet anyway. But the press in his heart to hold onto these moments was undeniable.

Katie bounded over, eyeing the pot roast.

"How were things at the General Store? Mrs. Yerby feeling better?" Ma moved back into the kitchen.

Oh yes, she *had* asked them to inquire after the store owner's wife. And they hadn't.

He looked at Katie and admitted, "We...um...forgot to ask."

"Forgot to ask?" Ma's eyes shone her confusion. True, it wasn't like him or Katie to be so remiss.

Katie frowned at her mother. "We were a little...distracted. Or at least David was."

He shot Katie a harsh look. If only he could rein in her tongue.

"Distracted? With what?" Ma set the cloths down and moved to the window. It was nearly quitting time for the ranch. Was she looking to see if Pa had come back in from the farther off pastures?

Katie was all innocence as she peered at her brother. Did she regret her admission? Even a little?

He offered an alternative, hoping she would relent. "It was nothing. Katie spotted Mary Foster."

"Ah. I do hope you had a good visit." Ma glanced at Katie.

"I did. But it wasn't as interesting as—"

David elbowed his sister.

"Ow!"

Ma jerked around.

Katie rubbed at her arm.

Ma's gaze landed on David.

He shrugged.

But her brow furrowed. She wasn't buying it.

"What is going on with you two?" Ma tsked before turning to check the coffee pot on the stovetop.

Katie glared at David with a pinched mouth. "David doesn't want you to know he talked to a man from the stagecoach about a job."

David had barely registered the sound of the front door opening just before her outburst. And he could not make himself turn around after.

"What's this about a job?" Pa's deep voice filled the house.

CHAPTER 3

Caught

David froze and then shifted his gaze toward the front door. The urge to shrink away from his father's angered expression was overwhelming. Indeed, he did take a step back.

Pa looked at each person in the room before settling on David. "Who here is in need of a job?" His words were hard, clipped.

David shot a pained expression at Katie.

She shrugged and looked away. Good...she should feel guilty for this mess she had gotten him into.

David cleared his throat. "Katie was only referring to a passing conversation."

"With...?" His father's eyes were expectant, not softening in the least.

David glanced at his mother.

She, too, seemed curious about what he would say. But her features gentled their lines. Ma would support him no matter what...wouldn't she?

"There was a man from the stagecoach company. He mentioned they were looking for able-bodied men."

Pa's eyebrows lifted. Was he curious? Or doubtful? "And why would he bother you?"

"I suppose because I'm an able-bodied man."

A nervous laugh escaped Katie.

Tossing her a look, David noticed that she bit at her lip and looked down as if that would disguise her ill-timed giggle.

Pa, too, glanced in her direction. Then back at David, letting out a long exhale. "That is that, I suppose. Can't fault a person for asking." He moved into the kitchen, pressing a kiss to the side of Ma's face.

As he pulled back, she swatted at him. "You need to wash up."

He waggled his brows in the way he only did with Ma.

David's face warmed and he looked away. It was endearing how his parents showed affection. But that didn't mean he had to like it.

Pa walked to the pump sink as Katie meandered to the dish cabinet and grabbed napkins.

"David," Ma entreated. "Can you bring the roast to the table?"

"Sure will." He nodded as he moved toward the stove, all too thankful to have dodged a potentially awkward conversation. Hopefully that would be the end of it.

But did he want it to be?

That surprised. He couldn't want that job, could he? Yet, he did.

His imagination had spun a dream of possibilities of life in the open—adventure and something new around every corner. His heart ached for his plight. Here he was, stuck in Cripple Creek at this ranch with limited opportunity, limited novelty, limited...everything.

Not to say that it didn't make a good living for his father. And not to say that his inheritance wasn't worth anything. It was. But was it for David? That, he didn't know.

Still, there was reason to keep the peace. He didn't want to distance his Pa. Besides, he wasn't one to tip the boat when it was perfectly sound as it was.

Setting the oversized pan in the middle of the table, he relished the delectable smells wafting toward him.

Ma patted his shoulder. "Thanks."

He gave her another quick nod.

"Shall we?" Pa came up behind Ma and indicated the dining chairs.

Everyone took their place and paused, folding hands and bowing heads.

Pa's voice, deep and sure, filled the room. "Heavenly Father, we thank You for Your many, many blessings—for the ranch, for this house, for Your plan for us, and for our family. I thank You for Your protection and provision. Please bless this food to our bodies and our hands into Your service. Amen."

The prayers lifted up around this table—be it from Pa or Ma—were always heartfelt and simple, and thick with meaning. David had to wonder if there was something to the enumerated blessings this evening. Not that it was out of character, but still, it seemed pointed. Or was David looking for it to be so?

David settled into his chair, leaning back. And decided to not dwell on it any longer. Pa wasn't a passive person. If he had a problem, he said it outright. No subterfuge.

Pa reached for Ma's plate as he stood, leaning over the pot roast and dishing her a generous helping.

She never ate as much as he gave her, but it didn't matter. His desire was for her to have plenty, he always said.

Then Pa served Katie, then David, before doling out his own food.

Pa's kind, servant-hearted ways struck David. It had been that way all their years, but it mattered all the same. He would not take it for granted.

Katie spoke up. "We ran into Mary Foster at the General Store."

David resisted the urge to roll his eyes. Katie had never been comfortable with silence, no matter how amiable it was.

"So you said earlier." Ma jabbed a piece of potato with her fork. "Mrs. Jones mentioned that her mother is not well. Is that so?"

Katie scrunched her face. "I didn't think to ask after her parents."

Ma didn't respond, just put the bite in her mouth.

David wasn't any more surprised than Ma. Katie wasn't as thoughtful as Ma about asking after family members. She was always too much in the moment. Unless anyone dared mention Ellie Mae. That's when she clammed up, dragged back into that horrid and unfortunate accident, stuck in the past.

But as David wanted to shake his head at his sister's oversight, he realized he hadn't asked either.

He, too, had heard that Mrs. Foster suffered with some manner of ailment. Hopefully, she had overcome it. But they —neither Katie nor he—hadn't asked. Did that make him uncaring? Or was it only that he avoided prolonging his conversation with Mary?

And why would that be? She was pleasant and warm, a bit shy true, but always kind.

"I talked to Mr. Foster a few days ago," Pa inserted. "He seemed to think she was improving."

Ma blotted her mouth with her napkin. "That's good news." Something in Ma's voice seemed hesitant. As if she didn't fully agree.

But no one questioned it. And David wondered if Mary's mother was in a bad way. If so, was Mr. Foster unwilling to speak of it?

He would have to remember to ask when he next saw Mary.

Pa muttered, "He is eager for that stage route to come through Cripple Creek."

Back to the stage. David frowned and tried to cover up any interest by shoving a forkful of meat into his mouth. Maybe too much. He reached for his water glass.

"It can only be good for the bank," Ma said between bites.

Of course. Mr. Foster would think anything that helped the bank and his employer, Mr. Hammond, was a great idea.

"But will it be good for the rest of us?" Pa threw the statement out to them all.

"We'll get supplies sooner," David offered.

Pa looked to David, his expression unreadable. "What have we needed that the General Store or blacksmith hasn't had? Or been able to secure?"

David knew he shouldn't continue, but he did. "I only meant that we won't have to wait as long for the things we need."

"That is a small inconvenience." Pa shifted his focus back to the food on his plate.

David wanted to argue. There had been times they needed things—rope, fabric, iron, whatever—and had to wait. It hadn't caused a major setback...yet. But why should they have extended waits when there was the possibility of eliminating such?

Pa shrugged. "I'm not opposed to progress, but it can affect our lives in more ways than you think."

David wanted to scoff and barely held back his reaction. Pa had never been eager for progress, always wanting things to remain as they were. Never a proponent for change. Why should this be any different? "What of Dr. Shaffer? Think of what a wonderful thing it will be for him to have more ready access to medicines."

Pa nodded but did not remove his attention from his plate. "That may be true." Then he met David's gaze. "But the stage will bring more than that—more visitors, for one. And what manner of folks will it be?"

"Should we really worry about what *might* happen? Or let it keep us from embracing what will *certainly* happen?" David flung the words without thinking.

Pa's eyes widened. "Spoken like someone who has great interest in the stage."

David jerked his shoulders, wishing he could shrug off the intensity of Pa's stare. Clearing his throat, David then continued, "I just think we shouldn't oppose something based on random fears. Not when the possibilities for good—real good—is well established."

Pa set his fork down and steepled his fingers. "Ah..." The word was dragged out as if Pa were merely appeasing a small child.

David couldn't back down now. "And what would it matter if I see the potential?"

Pa's eyebrows rose. "The potential for the town? Or the potential for *you*?"

David shifted in his seat. The urge to push on pressed him, but he didn't want to cause more tension. Though tense is how this exchange had become. Still, at this point, what did he have to lose? He jutted out his chin and returned Pa's gaze. "Why can't it be both?"

Ma inhaled sharply.

David felt both her and Katie's glare. But he dared not so much as glance in their direction. He couldn't back down. Not now.

"So you admit...you have an interest in the stage after all." Pa's voice became louder.

Everything in David wished to crawl out of his skin and

wriggle away. Not a chance; he was a man. It was time to start acting like one.

Clenching his teeth, he pushed out a breath. "Maybe I do."

Pa's fork clanged against his plate and his arms stiffened. "You would leave the ranch? Leave everything you have here? To chase after a...a blind hope for something better?"

Ma set a hand to Pa's forearm. He didn't so much as flinch.

David stood. "I would chase the chance to stand on my own two feet, to be someone in this world. Someone other than a rancher's son."

Ma gasped. "Katie, go to your room."

Pa's gaze deepened and his mouth twitched. His eyes became as steel. "If you don't want this life, I won't stop you." There was something more beneath his curt words. Something that felt more pained.

"David—" Ma fumbled with her words. "Don't do anything rash."

David couldn't move. What was he to do? Run off into the night? Go to town and find the stagecoach owner? He may have already been too hasty. Still, he pushed back his chair and said, "I think it's time for me to go."

Pa stood. "Thank you for the meal, Lauren. I've just lost my appetite." Then he rose, turned, and moved off in the direction of the stairs.

David's muscles ached with held tension. He wanted to take it back, but yet he didn't. Because he wouldn't mean it if he did. He truly felt what he had said.

Ma was suddenly on her feet and coming around the table. "David..."

He backed away from her. The last thing a man needed was his mother coddling him. "I'll leave in the morning. If I might presume I can still bed here tonight." He watched her stricken expression.

Her lips became a thin line. "You are always..." Emotion choked out her words. "Just think about what you're doing." She reached for his arm.

He pulled away. "I have made my decision." Stepping clear of the dining area, he strode to the front door.

And as he closed the door firmly, he leaned against the frame. All the fight had left him. What had he done? It was brash, but he had meant every word.

Should he go back inside and apologize? Somehow make it better?

But he couldn't. Because it wasn't all right. Everything was changing, had been changing within him for some time. Now everyone knew.

He decided he'd bed down in the barn tonight and head to town in the morning. On his own.

Mary propped her mother up as she moved her in the direction of the clinic. The ride to town had been trying. As had the process of getting mother out of the wagon. Thank the Lord the livery owner had been there to assist her or she might never have managed. But the larger man had made it look easy. Too bad he wouldn't be able to help when Mary got home. But she didn't want to think about that right now.

First, she had to conquer this doctor visit, which her mother was only somewhat aware of. Then she had to figure out the rest. That would come in its time.

"We're almost there," she said to her mother, hoping it encouraged rather than condescended. The latter would not be well received.

Ma stumbled, but Mary had a firm hold on her arm.

Though in an attempt to right herself, Ma jabbed an elbow into Mary with a bit of force.

Mary winced but didn't pull back. She wouldn't risk Ma falling. How was the woman still so dizzy? She'd ensured that Ma got a full breakfast. This only served to increase Mary's concern and eagerness to hear what Dr. Shaffer had to say. Except that she was equally nervous about the doctor's assessment. What if Ma had something terribly wrong? What if it wasn't a matter of just getting her to eat?

"Where are we going?" Ma huffed out.

It must be trying for her—struggling to put one foot in front of the other, a task that was second nature to grown folks.

"We are almost there." Mary hoped Ma wouldn't discern that she avoided answering.

They approached the clinic door and Mary knocked.

Ma stared at the door. "The clinic? Are we paying a call to Dr. Shaffer?"

Mary grimaced. How was she to sidestep that query? "I need to speak with him about something."

"Perhaps I can sit out here." Ma shifted toward the bench just outside the door.

Mary gripped her more tightly. "Maybe we both best go in. Dr. Shaffer may have questions."

Ma didn't appear to be convinced, but she stopped trying to pull free.

The door opened and Dr. Shaffer frowned. "Mrs. Foster, Mary, did we have an appointment this morning?"

Mary's face warmed. "No, sir. I hoped you might have a few moments to spare."

The physician's aged features lifted slightly. "As a matter of fact, I do have a half hour before my next patient."

Mary let out a breath. So far, so good.

Dr. Shaffer moved back to allow the women to pass into the area that served as his office and exam room.

Mary urged Ma forward. The woman peered about as if she hadn't been in the clinic before. It was odd. But so were many things with Ma these days.

"Mrs. Foster, why don't you sit over here." Dr. Shaffer indicated the exam table.

Ma glared at him, then at Mary. "What is this? Are we here for me?"

There was nowhere else to hide. "I have a couple of questions for Dr. Shaffer about what's been ailing you."

"Me? I feel fine."

Mary narrowed her gaze and frowned. "There's no need to hide this. You haven't been well for a while. I just want to know what could be the cause. How else can we help you."

Dr. Shaffer's eyebrows lifted. "Still hasn't been well? No improvement then?"

Mary tugged Ma toward the raised table. "She hasn't wanted to tell anyone. We both hoped it would pass. But it hasn't. In fact, it seems worse."

Dr. Shaffer came alongside Ma from the other side and helped Mary get her onto the table. He reached for his medical instruments and began his exam. First listening to her heart and having her breathe deeply. "What seems to be the issue?"

"She sleeps quite a bit of late. It's becoming more and more difficult to wake her. And she is dizzy and confused often." Mary choked out the words past a lump forming in her throat. She hated to expose Ma's weaknesses, but they needed help. Real help. And answers.

Dr. Shaffer focused on Ma as he peered into her eyes and ears. "Everything seems to be in order."

"We also have noticed more...challenges come on when she hasn't eaten."

Dr. Shaffer's gaze shifted to Mary. There was something

beyond his stark expression...something troubled. "How about her liquid intake?"

"She is taking in plenty, but she still always seems to be thirsty."

Then he turned to Ma. "Do you find you need to relieve yourself more often?"

Ma shook her head.

"She does," Mary insisted. "But I thought it was because she was drinking so much."

His features tightened. "I see."

The lump in Mary's throat grew, creating an uncomfortable pressure. What was Dr. Shaffer thinking? He appeared to be chasing a thought.

"I beg your pardon," he said as he looked between the two women. "But I would like to speak with Mr. Foster."

Mary's features heated. She couldn't bring Pa here. She couldn't let him know that she had sought out the doctor without his knowing. "He...is rather busy these days. Mr. Hammond needs him more often of late at the bank."

Dr. Shaffer's expression hardened. "I really think I need to wait until he can be here."

Mary's heart raced. "What is it? Is something terribly wrong?"

Ma's features slackened. Even she must sense something was afoot. "What is it, Dr. Shaffer? What is happening to me?"

The physician rubbed a hand across his face. Then looked between them again. "I am not comfortable speaking on the matter without Mr. Foster present." He pushed out a breath. "But I will."

Mary relaxed a bit. She didn't like the doctor's reluctance and hated that she had come without Pa's knowledge. But something had to be done. *Please, Lord, please let all be well!*

Dr. Shaffer looked pointedly at Ma. "I believe you are suffering from diabetes mellitus."

"Diet-bee-tis?" Ma tried to say the word. "What is that?"

"I'm sorry to say, ma'am, but there is much we don't know. Actually, there are more questions than we have answers."

That didn't sound good.

Ma gasped. "Is it...fatal?"

The doctor shifted. "Not necessarily." An obvious evading of the question.

"What does that mean?" Mary blurted. She pulled back and worked to press down her rising apprehension.

"It seems that the condition can be helped by monitoring diet. More meat and dairy...not as much bread and potatoes and the like."

"That sounds easy enough." Mary didn't understand the doctor's earlier hesitation and his concern if it was that simple.

"I must be forthcoming, though. Many still struggle with problems—losing eyesight, trouble with extremities—such as toes and fingers—and...other challenges."

Mary desperately wanted to know what these 'other challenges' were, but she struggled to swallow these other things. Might Ma become blind? What were these foot and hand troubles? Would she go numb? Lose her fingers and toes? What was he not saying?

She opened her mouth to broach the questions rolling through her mind.

But Dr. Shaffer held up a hand, stopping her before she started. "Again, there is much we don't understand about diabetes mellitus. And I really don't wish to say more without your father present."

Mary blinked. What was he not wanting to tell them? How was she to tell Pa that she'd brought Ma to the clinic without his knowledge? How could she best share the doctor's vague words? And how would she ever convince him to come speak with Dr. Shaffer?

The overwhelming prospect weighed on her, rendering her speechless.

"I know it's a lot to take in. Perhaps we should plan a time when Mr. Foster can come in and we will talk more."

Mary nodded, numbly.

"For now," he said, looking to Ma, "Let's focus on eating animal fats and meats only. Maybe some milk and cheese."

"Yes, doctor." Mary reached for her mother to assist her down from the table.

Dr. Shaffer, likewise, grabbed for Ma's other arm.

Once she was on her own two feet, Mary came alongside her again. "Thank you, Dr. Shaffer."

Ma didn't say anything to the man. Because she was off in her own world again? Or because she was likewise overwhelmed?

As Mary moved toward the clinic door, her heart sank. How would they get through this?

David stepped into the General Store. Where could that stage recruiter be? He still felt sick thinking about how he had left the ranch with little a word to anyone. And how he had avoided his father. It felt wrong... probably because it was.

He pushed that from mind and scanned the store. This was not the time to dwell on what was. For now it just was. Nothing he could do about it except go groveling back to his father. And what would that gain him? A place on the ranch permanently. He wasn't certain that was for him. Not anymore.

"Something I can help you with?" Mr. Yerby called in his direction, scattering his thoughts.

David shook his head. "Thanks. I'm looking for someone." Then he turned.

"Anyone I know?"

David paused. Should he make it known in town that he sought a job with the stagecoach? Perhaps it didn't matter. It wasn't as if folks wouldn't find out soon enough. "There was a recruiter for the stage visiting with Mr. Hammond about town yesterday. Any chance you've seen them today?"

Mr. Yerby took a moment to answer. Was he trying to decide what David wanted with the man? Or intended? At length, he did speak. "Ah...I think I did see them. Might have been headed in the direction of Mrs. Abby's café."

David tipped his hat. "Thanks."

Mr. Yerby nodded and turned toward an approaching customer. "Mrs. Smith, what a beautiful bolt of fabric."

David sighed. At least Mr. Yerby hadn't questioned him further. Not that the man was oblivious. David would wager he had put two and two together well enough and opted to not say anything on the matter. Not that it was his business anyway.

Moving back outside, he squinted against the sun. These chilly days would not last long. Not with such intense light bearing down on them.

He turned to the right and stopped short. There stood Mary Foster and her mother.

Mary inhaled as if fearful he would run into her. Indeed, she held more tightly to her mother.

He tipped his hat. "Good day, Mary, Mrs. Foster."

"And a fine day to you as well." Mrs. Foster smiled. "What brings you to town?"

Goodness, must everyone be so interested in his movements? "I...ah...have business with Mr. Hammond's friend."

Mary's eyes widened.

And David remembered...a bit too late. She had been there yesterday when the stage recruiter spoke with him. He dipped his head, wanting to avoid her gaze. That seemed silly, though, for it wasn't as if he could truly disappear. She was directly in front of him.

So he looked up and caught her eyes. There was surprise

there, yes, but something more...saddened. What was that about? It tugged at his heart. Why should that be?

"Such a fine young man you have become." Mrs. Foster's voice intruded. "Don't you think, Mary? Why, I must be certain to tell your Ma what a fine fellow she has raised. How is she these days?"

David dropped his gaze to his boots. He didn't want to think on his mother right now. Certainly not at the angst in her eyes as he left not even an hour ago. It had been almost more than he could bear to walk away from. Dwelling on it would not help matters. "She's...well."

"Oh good. Such a kind family you have. Always ready to help when needed." The woman's eyes watered. Had she a story of Ma or Pa stepping in to assist? It gave him a moment of pause. Mrs. Foster was right. His parents hadn't a selfish bone between the two of them.

He licked his lips, which were suddenly dry, and tried not to give in to the draw to look at Mary. "They are fortunate to have such considerate friends."

The older woman patted Mary's arm. "Such a gentleman. Don't you think, Mary?" The look she passed to her daughter seemed to bear more than what he could see.

David wasn't quite sure what was being communicated, but it was clear something was. "What brings you two to town?"

Mrs. Foster frowned at Mary as she squirmed a bit. As if she didn't wish to say. Had he trespassed? "We need some things from the General Store."

"Ah." Though he was a bit confused as Mary had just come yesterday. Had she not gotten everything she needed? Unable to fight the urge any longer, his gaze slid toward her.

She looked to the side and bit at her lip. Was she so out of sorts?

Not that he had the first clue how to speak to a woman's

troubles. He barely held his own with Katie and Ma. He in no way could read a woman well enough to imagine he'd say the right thing.

He'd best excuse himself before things got worse.

"It's been nice chatting, but I need to find Mr. Hammond." He purposefully didn't mention Mr. Green. No sense confusing the situation any further.

"Of course." Mrs. Foster tapped Mary's arm again. "Give my regards to your parents."

Mary looked at him as if she wanted to say something, but her mother shuffled forward, tugging her along.

As they passed him, Mary's arm came within inches of his. As usual, her presence warmed him. But also stirred some manner of concern. Something wasn't well with her. Was it the fact he searched for Mr. Green? She certainly knew why. Was that what it was?

He shook his head to clear his thoughts. No sense in chasing that rabbit. He'd never be able to pin down the female mind anyway, no matter how much he tried. So it was best to leave it be. Besides, he needed all his wits about him for the upcoming conversation with Mr. Green.

Moving past the General Store and toward the café, he rehearsed his words in his mind. How was he to go about this? What was the right thing to say?

Before he knew it, he stepped into the eatery.

Mrs. Abby was just then passing by the front door. She smiled and greeted him. "Need a table?"

He shook his head and took his hat off. "I'm looking for Mr. Hammond. He should have come in with another gentle-man." Even as he spoke, he scanned the tables within.

Mrs. Abby frowned. "I just took them their lunch. Did they plan for you to join them? They're at a table for two."

He waved a hand. "Nothing of the sort. I have business with Mr. Hammond's guest. It will only take a moment."

Her features held a skeptical expression. She did not like things upsetting her balance. And clearly someone joining her guests with no place to sit did not settle well with her.

He almost told her he would wait outside, but the trepidation growing within made him think he might just lose his nerve if he did. "This won't take long," he reiterated.

She sighed and held up a hand in the direction of the far wall. "Suit yourself." Then she stepped in the direction of the next table.

As she indicated, he spotted the men by the far wall. They were deep in conversation and well into their meals. Maybe it would be better if he waited. But the obstacles he had encountered thus far, driving him to question his decision, would no doubt compound if he had time to think on it.

So he marched across the dining room and straight to their table.

The men paused mid-sentence, forks just beyond their mouths.

Unable to stop himself, David blurted, "Mr. Green, I'd like to take that job with the stage."

Mary rushed her mother through the General Store. She had no patience for perusing the aisles and no desire for others to become more aware of Ma's confused state. She pressed for her mother to collect what they needed and move on.

Nodding to Mr. Yerby as they exited after settling up, she half pulled Ma along.

"Why the rush, dear? Maybe we'll come across that handsome friend of yours again."

Mary closed her eyes and pushed out a breath. That was the last thing she wanted—another opportunity to display her complete lack of ability to rein in her emotions. What he must think of her!

"He is rather nice, don't you think?" There was a lilt to Ma's voice.

Yes, Ma was definitely insinuating something. And Mary was not about to appease her inference.

"We need to get home before it's too late. Pa would be more pleased if supper is on the table when he gets home."

Ma frowned. "Certainly. But you don't want a chance to speak to your friend? You hardly said two words to him."

As a fact, Mary wasn't sure she said anything. His announcement that he sought out the stage recruiter had thrown her off balance. David wanted to leave Cripple Creek? Had something happened at home? Did he not want to run the Stoneybrook Ranch? Was there nothing to keep him here?

"Mary?" Her mother's voice grated. The woman could be rather insistent. "Didn't you have a care for him?"

Mary jerked toward her mother. "Ma! That isn't true!" She glanced about to see who might have heard. But they had moved well beyond the bustle near the mercantile. They were almost to the livery, but not quite close enough for anyone there to overhear.

Ma harrumphed. "That's not how it appeared last Sunday. At least not to me."

Was that true? Was Mary so obvious? Did others know?

Her face heated. "Let's get you home. David is itching to leave Cripple Creek, so there's nothing for it even if I were interested."

"Leave Cripple Creek?" Ma said on an intake of air. "What gives you such an idea as that?"

Mary grimaced. She hadn't meant to say that. But she'd let it slip. Could she distract Ma? "I just mean, he has grand ideas of what the future could hold."

"Yes. But he wouldn't walk away from the ranch. Not a

chance. That would be senseless. And he needs a helpmate to keep the house."

Mary nearly let out a growl. "That doesn't mean he's interested in me filling that role. Now, let's stop talking such nonsense and get on home." *Please, Lord*, she prayed. *Please let her not dwell on this.*

Her heart was wounded enough as it was. He had never been able to see her. Not truly. What could she do? She wasn't a flirt like Betsy Callaway. And the boys didn't seem to care for her more quiet nature.

Except...David had always been kind to her. Always seemed amiable. It was one of the things that drew her to him. That, and his good looks—strong, chiseled features, light brown hair, amber eyes that were both deep and caring, and a sense of goodness about himself. What was there not to like?

For certain, many of the girls they had been in school with would take his offer of marriage were it to be given. That, however, did not seem likely—not for them, and not for her. How was he supposed to notice her when she could hardly string a few sentences together in his presence?

She was hopeless.

Ma called for the livery owner. Only then did Mary notice how close they had come to the stables. My, she could get lost in her thoughts.

In a matter of moments, she and Ma were loaded in the wagon—thanks to the livery owner's help—and Mary directed the horse toward their home.

They rode most of the way in silence; Ma seemed rather spent after being helped into the driver's box, and Mary did not wish to encourage conversation. Why would she? She didn't want Ma asking more questions she couldn't answer.

Soon enough, however, they pulled up to the cabin Mary had always called home. Now was the trial of getting Ma down and into the house.

"Wait until I come around," Mary called to her mother as she managed her own way to the ground. As her feet hit the earth, she took in a deep breath and let it out, trying to release her worries. It did not help, her thoughts continued to swirl about her.

Regardless, she couldn't leave Ma aloft. So she walked around the front of the cart, soothing the well-mannered gray mare with a quick rub down her nose before she came to the other side.

"What are you doing?" Ma grumbled.

"I am going to help you down." Mary's voice was weak, even to her ears.

"You? By yourself?" Ma shot her an incredulous look. "I would do better on my own, I think. With both of us, there will likely be injury."

Mary bit back her immediate response. Chiding mother would serve neither of them. After she drew in another cleansing breath, she said, "All the same, I think it best we attempt it as a team."

Ma's brows drew together. This was not going to go well.

Just then the sound of hoofbeats echoed through the stillness. Who came?

Mary peered around the wagon to see Pa coming on his Appaloosa. She released a long sigh. She wouldn't have to put herself to the test today.

Then she had a thought. What would she tell Pa about their outing today? Would he be angry?

Pushing that to the side for later, she waved at him.

He tipped his hat and urged more speed from his horse. And in a few moments, he was coming around the wagon.

"What goes here?" His voice was a bit gruff.

"We made a trip to town. And I do not want Ma to injure herself getting down."

"So you thought to put yourself at risk?" He dismounted.

How was it that her parents, such very different people, had such similar ways of thinking?

Pa brushed past Mary and lifted his arms toward his wife.

Mary stepped back and watched, helpless, as Pa struggled to get Ma on firm ground. At length, and with no shortage of effort, they succeeded.

"Now get your Ma into the house while I tend to the horses," Pa said, reaching for the gray mare's bit.

Mary nodded and came alongside her mother, assisting her up the stairs. Once they entered the house, she settled Ma at the dining table.

"What shall we make for supper?" Ma asked, not at all minding that she sat.

"*We* are not making anything. *I* will get started on something."

"But, you cannot—"

"I can. And I will. You need your rest."

Ma appeared as if she were prepared to argue but did not.

Pleased she wouldn't be further delayed, Mary moved into the kitchen and began chopping vegetables.

It wasn't long before Pa came inside. By then the vegetables and some beef stewed in a pot.

"Smells wonderful." Pa looked between Mary and Ma. What must he think? Did he know where they had been?

"You're home early," Mary said, keeping her attention on the pot unnecessarily.

"Mr. Hammond asked me to go to Victor this morning. And by the time I returned, he had closed down for the day. So I came home." There was a twinkle in Pa's eye. It worried Mary just enough to distract her.

He no longer seemed concerned about her and Ma's trip to town. Should she come out with the truth of it though? Clear the air?

"Did you two have a pleasant outing?"

Mary gripped the lid of the pot, feeling the heat through the cloth to her hand. She jerked it away. "Ah, yes."

The guilt ate at her. She had never been a rebellious or disobedient child, always finding honesty and integrity to be the easier road.

"We saw Dr. Shaffer today," Ma said as Pa eased into a dining chair.

He paused before settling. "You what?" A sharp look pierced the space between the dining room and the kitchen.

Mary set her wooden spoon down and stepped to the table. "I was so worried, Pa. I had to go. I had to know. I'm sorry for going against you."

He held up a hand. "It is no matter, dear." Sitting finally, he rubbed a thumb across the table in front of him. "I wish you had asked me first, but I do know how you fret."

She released a breath. That hadn't been bad at all. He had been rather...understanding. That gave rise to even more concern. "You're not angry then?"

"No. On my ride to Victor, I began to reconsider my words yesterday. I, too, worry, you know."

Mary nodded. She didn't doubt that for a moment.

"So, what did Dr. Shaffer say?" Pa didn't look the least bit concerned.

Mary blew out a breath. "He said that Ma has diabetes mellitus. That we need to make sure she gets plenty of animal fat and meats. Less breads and grains."

Pa bobbed his head. "And that will cure her?"

"No," Mary confessed. "There is little hope of that. We can only manage her diet and any other problems that arise."

He set his hands on the table. "Well, I have something that will fix that."

"Fix it? What do you mean? Didn't you understand what I said?"

Pa smiled and looked at Mary as if she were a small child

who couldn't comprehend. "I came across a man on my trip today."

Mary lowered her eyebrows. "A man?"

"A man selling medicine. A 'cure for what ails' is what he said."

"How is that possible? If such a thing existed wouldn't Dr. Shaffer know about it?"

Pa stood and went back to the saddlebag that Mary hadn't noticed he'd brought in. He opened the flap and extracted a bottle of brown liquid.

"An elixir." Pa held the bottle's label toward her. "Guaranteed it to work for any problems."

She moved closer and, sure enough, the label read 'Ethan's Tonic: An Elixir For What Ails.'

"Can we trust this? What's in it?"

"I'm not sure. After all, I'm not a doctor. But he had a man traveling with him that had been on his death bed with consumption. A glass of the elixir every day cured him."

That didn't sound right. The best doctors in the country had no way to cure consumption.

"So I bought a bottle. It is just what we need to fix your Ma right up."

Mary wasn't so sure. But she wasn't a doctor either. Nor could she defy her father when he had an idea such as this. So she bit her lip and watched Pa grab a glass from the cabinet and pour some of the thick liquid into it. Then handed it to Ma.

CHAPTER 5

Leaving

David looked at the bag he had prepared. Of all the things on the ranch, these were his possessions. Well, the only ones he was able to take. Many of the things in his room didn't truly belong to him. At least, he would feel guilty taking them. And other things...there just wasn't room in his bag. He had precious little space to take personal items...necessities were of the utmost importance.

Glancing about the room at the things that had filled his waking moments, he sighed. He had never imagined what it would be like to leave this room, this house for the rest of his life.

An anchor sunk in his midsection. Was that really what it was? After Pa's reaction, he wouldn't doubt if the man would not welcome him back.

"What are you doing?" a voice pressed from behind.

He spun around to find Katie leaning on the door frame, watching him. How long had she been there?

Grabbing the clothing he had gathered on the bed, he shoved the small stack into the bag. "What does it look like?"

Gentle footfalls belied that she stepped within the room. "You know what I mean. This has gone on long enough."

He ignored her, moving to the shelf in the opposite corner and making a show of setting knick knacks in their place.

Her tone became pleading. "Just apologize to Pa. I know he'll forgive you."

He jerked his head around, pinning her with his gaze. "It's not about that."

"Isn't it?" She crossed her arms over her chest.

"No." He looked out the nearby window. Pa was out there with the ranch hands, doing what he did every day to sustain the place. And David didn't want to be here when he came back. It would be best if he had taken his leave. "You think this is just about an apology? That I misspoke?"

"Didn't you?"

He shook his head. How could he make her understand? "Katie, it's much more. Something pressing within me to take hold of what's out there," he said, jabbing a finger toward the window and the world beyond. Indeed there was opportunity aplenty. He just had to grab his chance—a chance to leave this ranch, this town, and...

And what? Find his own way? That sounded trite. But he had no other words. So, he straightened and faced her again. "I just...have to do this."

She dropped her regard to the floor. Was she so hurt by his decision?

He stepped to her and set a hand on her shoulder. "I'm not abandoning you. I'm still your brother, and you'd better believe I'll be checking in on you."

She peered up through eyelashes that had become moistened. Was she crying? In the next moment, she launched herself into his arms. "You'd better."

He let his sister embrace him. And though he told himself

it was for her sake, he knew that wasn't totally true. He would miss her.

After several breaths, he pulled back. "Now, you'd best not make trouble for Ma. She has enough on her plate."

Katie rolled her eyes. "I don't make trouble."

One eyebrow lifted, he gave her a lopsided smile.

"Oh, okay...enough with that. I'll do my best."

He chuckled. "That's all I ask."

Then he gathered his overfull bag and walked past her.

"Are you planning to talk to Ma before you go?"

He paused. That wasn't something he looked forward to. How could he bear the weight of her disapproval? Of her hurt? It had nearly split his heart in two when he'd told her of the arrangements he'd made with the stage recruiter. How could he face her now?

But he had to. It was unthinkable that he might slip away without saying goodbye.

He grimaced. "Of course I will." Then he moved in the direction of the stairs. He'd have to be quick about it if he wanted to make his exit before Pa returned to the house. Fair or not, he could not face the man again.

Taking the stairs as quickly as possible, the thought occurred to him that he'd left Katie in his room—his private space. He almost halted and called for her to get out his room one last time. Yet he couldn't make the words come out.

It wasn't his room anymore.

When he dropped off the last step, the clanging of dishes in the kitchen halted.

He closed his eyes and tried to clear his mind enough to pray. It was no use.

"David?" Came Ma's voice, heavy with emotion.

He stepped around the stairway, now fully visible to her. And forced himself to look at her.

She stood near the dining table, wringing a towel. Her

features were strained as she watched him. Would there be tears from her too? Could he bear it if there weren't?

"Ma..." The word was choked out.

Her gaze seemed to take him in. As if she wanted to hold the moment. Whatever for? This was the hardest thing he'd ever done.

She moved toward him and he almost flinched. But he held himself straight and called upon strength he didn't know he had left.

Now she was an arm's length away.

"So, you're really leaving?" Her words held more thickness than he'd have imagined possible.

He nodded, not trusting his tongue.

She reached out a hand and touched his arm. "I should have known this day might come. But I..." Her words were swallowed up in the tightness of her voice. "But I still hoped it wouldn't."

What could he say to that? Though her eyes entreated him to explain himself.

"I just...have to do this."

She nodded and looked at his bag. And sniffled.

How was he going to keep it together?

"Will you write?" The request was a plea.

"As I can." He tried to keep his tone even.

"And...will you talk to your Pa before you go?"

He frowned. "I...don't think I'll have time."

Her eyes widened. "Truly?"

She had him there. His decision was more about his inability to face the man he had obviously let down. The man who had probably disowned him.

Setting her hands on his arms, she took in a breath, then said, "David, your Pa is hurting too. He doesn't always know how to show it. But he is."

Her words sliced through him. How was he to hold it together with such talk?

He looked past her and toward the barn, visible from the kitchen window. "I...have to go."

She bit at her lip. And nodded. As if she didn't expect anything more or less than his refusal. Had she lost all faith in him?

Then again, he wasn't prepared to acquiesce. He could not look his father in the face. Not today. Maybe not ever again.

He firmed his stance and took a step back from the woman who had given him life, who had cared for him all of his days. "I'd...better get going."

She nodded. "Take care. And know I'm praying for you. Every single day."

He clamped his lips together. There was nothing more to say. Nothing more he could say and still hold it together.

So he leaned forward, brushed his lips across his mother's cheek, and walked out of the house.

Mary watched her parents just ahead of her as they strolled toward the church. They were sweet, holding hands and moving in step with one another. First, it reminded Mary of just how much improved her mother had become. Due to the tonic? Or the careful monitoring of her eating? Perhaps both, Mary conceded.

Pa leaned toward Ma and whispered something for her ears alone. She chuckled in response. Would Mary ever have such a companionable marriage? Would she be so fortunate to enjoy the connection her parents did? And, after all these years, they were still so devoted to each other.

Ma paused and looked back at Mary. "Something amiss?"

Mary shook her head. "No. Just relishing the view."

Ma inclined her face toward the mountains in the distance. "Ah, yes. Such a fine prospect."

Mary wanted to share that it was not the mountains that had so enraptured her, but she held back and once again considered how her father doted on his wife.

An image of David flashed in Mary's mind. Would he ever be so taken with her? He certainly wasn't at present. It almost seemed as if he barely noticed her. Much less had a deeper care. Not to the extent she hoped.

Sighing, she clasped her hands in front of her hips and picked up her step to catch her parents, who had walked several paces ahead. As she closed the gap, they entered the throng of church-goers gathered around the entrance.

Mary smiled to several of the townsfolk as she searched. For who? As if she didn't know.

Katherine Matthews waved from the far side of the crowd.

Mary smiled back, though she still scanned for Katie's brother. But to no avail. Had he not come to church today? Was he currently engaged in conversation with another young lady?

A sadness flowed through Mary. But she pushed it to the side. There was no reason for it. David wasn't hers—never had been. And if she couldn't find a way to be more...something, he never would be. How could she be more approachable? She had tried. But when he was near, her nerves sent her senses to skittering and her tongue thickened.

Katie stepped in the direction of the church's door, arm looped through her mother's. Mrs. Matthews looked more sullen than usual. Had something happened to David?

Mary's heart stuttered. Had he spoken to Mr. Green about leaving Cripple Creek? What if it was something more? What if he had been injured on the ranch?

She couldn't follow that thought. For certain, Katie and

Mrs. Matthews wouldn't be strolling through the church yard if something tragic had befallen their family.

A hand took hold of Mary's arm. She jerked her regard in that direction. But it was only Ma. Had she stepped away from Pa? He was farther along, speaking with Mr. Hammond and Mr. Green.

"What is it?" Mary asked, finding her Ma wide-eyed and tight lipped. Again, her heartbeat jumped, worried of what news she might bear.

Ma tugged Mary from the collecting group.

"Ma, you're scaring me." Indeed, she could hardly contain her trepidation.

Ma halted and drew Mary near. "Mr. Hammond and his friend mentioned that they have been recruiting for the stage."

This, Mary knew. She let out a breath. "Is that so?"

"Yes." Ma peered about. To ensure they weren't overheard? "And they filled their last position with David Matthews."

Though she should have expected it, Mary's heart seemed to stop and she couldn't quite catch her breath. He was gone. Would the stage company put him on a route far away? Had he left Cripple Creek for good then? A thickness filled her throat.

Ma looked at her expectantly, but Mary doubted she could speak. Ma's gaze softened and her lips settled into a frown. She was concerned. That much was evident. Did she know the full depth of Mary's care for David? Surely, she must.

Her grip tightened, not painfully so, but firmed yet. "Are you well?"

Mary nodded even as she set a hand to her midsection. How could this disturb her so? It wasn't as if he were her beau. This was ridiculous.

Ma's fingers gentled and stroked Mary's forearm. "It will be all right." Her tone was easy and soothing. "It will be."

Mary's eyes watered. How much more would she fall into this hurt? This was much more of a reaction than she would have expected from the small connection she'd had with David —friends at best, simply former schoolmates more likely.

"Still waters run deep, my dear." Ma touched the side of Mary's face. "You are stronger than you think."

Mary swiped at her eyes as she nodded.

Ma's hands clasped Mary's upper arms. "Take the time you need. Want me to wait with you?"

Mary shook her head. "I am well. I assure you. I...would like to find a seat."

Ma gave her a small smile.

"Mary," a voice called from closer to the church.

She looked up, hopeful that her eyes hadn't become puffy. Her father walked toward them with a younger man in tow.

Oh, Pa, not now! She could only stand and fret as the pair drew nearer. Throwing an urgent look in her mother's direction, she bit at her lip. But her mother had no control over the situation. No more than she.

She could run the other way...or she might could ask her mother make an excuse for her. Either appealed, but neither seemed plausible.

So, she did nothing but stand, rooted to the spot, as her father fairly dragged the younger man in their direction.

"Jonas, this is my wife. And this..." Pa held up a hand as if to present a prize. "...is my daughter Mary."

To Jonas's credit, he didn't appear as if he didn't wish to be introduced, though Mary could only describe his movements as coerced. He bowed slightly and took Mary's hand, his grip firm. "It is a pleasure to meet you, miss." Then he turned to Ma. "And you, Mrs. Foster."

Ma set a hand on Pa's arm. "What a nice gentleman." Then she gave Mary a look that neither apologized nor consoled, but could best be described as opportunistic. What was that? One moment her mother seemed to understand her pain, the next, she urged Mary toward another man. That didn't sit well.

"It is good to meet you, Mr...." Only then did she realize Pa had not finished the introductions.

"Anderson." The young man smiled. A pleasant smile. One that boasted perfectly placed teeth.

She nodded her thanks. "Mr. Anderson."

Then the awkward silence settled in. She shot a look to her parents. Neither of which appeared the least bit interested in helping.

Mary cleared her throat. "And what brings you to Cripple Creek, Mr. Anderson?"

"Like so many, I have come in hopes of making my future...in gold."

She blinked. Gold? He was a prospector? He didn't look like any of the unkempt middle-aged men she had run across. Then again, the largest lode found in this region was by a younger man, who was now a legend in the whole of Colorado. It did happen—men struck it rich. It wasn't so far-fetched.

"How interesting," Ma spoke up. Would she truly be interested in her daughter being courted by a man who had such an uncertain future?

"You may find there is more than gold here in Cripple Creek." Pa winked at Mary.

Could the ground just open and swallow her right now? Her face warmed and she looked to the side.

A silence befell the small group.

They were rescued this time, however, and by Mr. Anderson. "I think the service is about to start." He waved a hand toward the front of the church. "If it isn't an imposition, I wondered if I might sit with you and your family."

She wanted to deny him. Nothing in her wanted to

become more acquainted with anyone right now, certainly not another man. Not while her heart was bruised.

Ma nudged her and gave her a meaningful look.

Turning back to Mr. Anderson, Mary smiled as much as she could force onto her features. "That would be nice."

And so, the four moved toward the church, Ma and Pa, arms linked, a few steps ahead, and she and Mr. Anderson trailing behind.

This was the makings of a very long Sunday morning.

What a mess...indeed. Mary plunged the last shirt into the water, scrubbing the stain hard against the washboard. The spot had been formidable, but she would win the battle. Pulling it out of the water, colored by lye soap and the dirt thus far removed, she examined the area just below collar.

And grimaced.

Would it never come out? She pressed the back of her hand to her forehead. For certain, she perspired. But this mar would not win.

What had made her so determined this day? It wasn't as if she had never lost the war to a food smear upon a piece of clothing. What made today different? Made this one so important?

She glanced across the meadow and frowned. Perhaps the bigger question was how she would go about erasing the mar upon her heart. How had she let something so small affect her so deeply? There had never been any promises—or even an overture—from David. Nothing in his manner had ever given her the impression that something beyond simple friendship existed...or ever could.

Then why this ache?

But she knew. She *had* hoped, *had* prayed...and had cared. Still did care...so much. Though why she had let her heart carry her away to such fanciful places as the dream of David, she did not know.

Staring at the water, she considered whether to give up on the stain or keep trying. Would the strain upon her heart be equally impossible to heal? Or would time soothe the hurt?

Thumping of hooves pulled her from her distraction. A rider approached.

She narrowed her eyes as she drew a hand up to block the sun from her vision. It would be quite early for Pa to return.

But as she looked closer, she noted that, while it was indeed a man upon the horse, he carried himself differently. Who could it be then?

She had the thought that she should go inside and get Ma, but she paused. There was something familiar about the man's movements. Something that made her wonder. Could it be...? But why would he be *here*?

Stealing a glance toward the house, she thought she caught sight of the kitchen curtain moving. Did Ma watch? Had she expected this visitor?

Mary sighed. Ma meant well, but her interference was becoming bothersome.

Now the rider was well within the range necessary to recognize him—Jonas Anderson.

He slowed and tipped his hat as he smiled.

She offered a slight wave before setting the shirt to the side —something to attend to later—and smoothed a hand over errant hair and down a mussed skirt.

"Hello, Mr. Anderson," she called as he reined in just short of her position.

"Good day, Miss Foster. How are you this fine afternoon?"

"I am quite well." She nodded and watched as he dismounted. "How might I help you?"

His eyes registered a moment of concern. "I came for supper. I know I'm early. I just...wondered if there might be anything I could assist with." He tethered his horse to the nearby porch railing.

Her brows furrowed. "Supper?" Had Ma or Pa asked him to come? And didn't bother to warn her? Indeed, they were a tiresome pair. If she didn't know any better, these frequent invites of Mr. Anderson as a dinner guest would make her think they pressed for something to happen here.

Mary realized she had continued to rub at her waistband though her hands were sufficiently dry. "How kind of you. Ma is in the house. Let me check with her."

Jonas stepped in her path. "No need to worry your mother." His jaw worked as if he were nervous, but he continued, "I wondered if there were anything I might help *you* with."

She jerked back a bit. "I thank you, but I was just finishing the wash."

He glanced in the direction of the bin. "And I see you have some left to do."

She followed his gaze and waved a hand. "It is nothing. Just a shirt with a stubborn stain."

He rolled up his sleeves. "Maybe some extra muscle would help?"

It was kind for him to offer. And rather curious. She did note strongly built forearms, now exposed.

Her breath stuttered. He was an attractive man. And kind.

He stepped around her and to the wash bin.

"That's not necessary," she started saying as she turned. "You don't need to worry with—"

But he picked up the shirt and peered over it, perhaps

looking for the spot. "Nothing to it. I'm happy to help." He settled his gaze on her once more.

This time, her heart seemed to skip a beat. It was good of him to step in and help. Maybe she should let him.

Tipping her head, she nodded and murmured her thanks.

He worked on the shirt and she couldn't help but admire the scene. This was women's work, but he took it on as if it were nothing. The woman who caught his eye would certainly be fortunate to have such a servant-hearted fellow.

Another glance her way, coupled with a soft smile, made her face heat. Could it be that she was that woman? Did she want to be?

Her heart protested, citing her deeper care for David. But maybe, just maybe this kind man could help her forget those feelings.

She stepped closer to Jonas and worked to resecure the drying laundry. It was unnecessary, but she couldn't just stand there and stare at him, could she?

"This really is a tough spot to remove." He held the shirt up.

It had faded a bit more, but it was still visible. She moved to his side. "It may be beyond saving."

He frowned. "It seems a perfectly good shirt."

She let out a breath.

"Perhaps it can be patched?"

She imagined a square of cloth not of this material just below the collar and let out a little laugh. That would be strange indeed.

His cheeks colored.

"Oh, I didn't mean to imply that your suggestion was—"

He smirked. "It would look...different."

Setting a hand to his forearm, she shook her head. "It's a fine thought. But I don't think Pa would wear it anymore."

He dropped the shirt. And stared at his arm. Or rather...at her hand upon it.

She hadn't realized...

Retracting her hand, she was surprised when he turned to face her. They were so close she could feel the heat radiating from him. "I...wondered, Miss Foster, if you might be interested in my taking you to supper at the café sometime?"

She widened her eyes. Was he truly interested in pursuing her? As a beau? Was she likewise open to such a connection?

Licking her lips, she considered her answer. That could very well be the path to opening her heart for something new. Something that may prove her healing.

As she looked up at him again, she sensed that his breathing had stopped. Did he hold it? Waiting her response?

The kitchen curtain again fluttered. Did Ma watch their interaction? Spy on her?

She swallowed. "I would like that very much."

He settled back into himself, his shoulders relaxing. "So would I."

She offered him a small smile. Perhaps this new pang in her heart was something taking root and preparing to blossom. Perhaps.

David gritted his teeth against the movement of the stagecoach over a rut. How was he not used to the roughness of these routes? Still, he urged the horses onward. They had to arrive at the station before sundown.

The man beside him shifted his shotgun to his other knee and leaned in. "Don't let the horses think you have any nerves about you. They can sense it."

David glanced at the more experienced driver who served

as his shotgun messenger on this, his last run before getting his own route.

Even though David likely had more familiarity with horses from his work on the ranch, he respectfully nodded and settled back. Indeed, he let out a breath and felt his shoulders relax.

"There you go," Hank encouraged. "Easy does it."

David gave him a brief nod and then focused on the animals in front of him. But he knew Hank had been right—David was tense. Though likely from more than the bumpiness of the road. For he drove this stagecoach into the heart of Cripple Creek.

But he was far from the prodigal returning home. He embraced his new adventure, this life away from his family. It was far from glamorous, this new life—sleeping in stations, not having a place of his own. In truth, it was perhaps a little lonelier than he'd anticipated. But he was living his dream.

Either way, he had less than no desire to see his father. Even if Pa would invite him in and forgive his rash exit a month past, he wouldn't bend. Wait...had it been that long?

Yes, it had. David left home quite nearly four weeks ago. What had he accomplished in that time? Had it been worth the hurt hearts and strained relationships?

He hated that he didn't have an answer for that. Not a clear answer at any rate.

A hand landed on his forearm.

"I said relax yourself, not the horses." Hank's words judged. Maybe too harshly.

But as David noted the horses' pace, he realized he had, indeed, slackened his control. He tightened his grip and prodded the animals to pick up speed.

Though as he glanced about, he saw the familiar landscapes that had always been home. No more.

He pushed that thought to the side also lest it cause him to err in his driving once more.

"You're doing fine." The encouragement from Hank was sorely needed. "We'll be there soon enough."

David hadn't needed the reminder. He was still torn about whether or not he should stop by Stoneybrook Ranch. Dare he go and face down his father? See his mother's pained expression? Isn't that what would happen? Not to mention that he would bear the brunt of Katie's anger. Was she still upset with him?

Maybe this wasn't the time to face them. That dismissive thought only caused guilt to trickle into his heart. Even more than that which he had held to since leaving. Would it never stop?

He shifted his hold on the reins and steered the animals toward the fast-approaching town. His time to make a decision was nearing its end. Still, he pressed his anticipation down and focused on the horses.

Driving them toward the center of Cripple Creek as the buildings came into full view, he couldn't help but wonder if any of his family members were about in town. If so, how would he avoid them?

Sighing, his grip became more tense as he pulled back to slow the animals.

In a matter of moments, with dust kicked up around the stagecoach, he brought the whole of it to a stop.

Hank clapped him on the shoulder. "I think you're ready, boy."

He offered the man a smile even though he didn't necessarily appreciate the fatherly, well-meaning condescension. So he only nodded before turning and dropping from the driver's bench.

Patting the spent horses down, he watched as Hank

opened the door for their passengers and spoke with the sheriff about the strongbox they had carried into Cripple Creek.

He scanned the area, looking and not looking for his family. And he expelled a great sigh when he hadn't noted anyone of importance. Although, he spotted a young man who he didn't know, speaking with a blonde woman at the nearby telegraph office. Why they should catch his attention, he didn't know. The woman's movements seemed somewhat familiar, but her features were denied him. The man was a complete stranger, perhaps the woman was too.

She removed her arm from his elbow and he smiled as she moved into the office.

David stepped onto the platform. Now only a few feet away, the stranger turned his dark eyes toward David.

"Hot one today," the rather young man tipped his hat.

"Yes, it is." David didn't need reminding, but he appreciated the consideration. "You new here? I can't say as I remember seeing you in Cripple Creek before."

A look of confusion passed over the man's features. Probably wondering why the stagecoach driver cared.

Still, the man stuck out his hand. "I'm recently moved here. Jonas Anderson."

David shook it. "David Matthews."

"Are you a regular driver to Cripple Creek?" Jonas asked.

Ah, there was the confusion. "I'm from this area. I grew up at Stoneybrook Ranch." Why did he feel the need to share such information? True, the man was easy to chat with, but that didn't mean he had to tell him everything. Certainly no more than the man needed to know. So David turned the conversation back around as he kept an eye on the bags being unloaded. "What brings you this way?"

"I'm a prospector. Looking to make my fortune, I suppose." The man laughed a little. At himself?

"Oh?" There had been many upon many prospectors to

this area in David's years. After a big lode made Winfield Scott Stratton a millionaire, more and more came, hoping to follow in his footsteps. "Best of luck to you."

Jonas looked toward the telegraph office where his companion had gone. "I...um...might be looking for more steady work. Know of anything in the area?"

David followed Jonas's gaze and bit back a smile. The man had intentions of settling down with his lady friend and making a life with her. David couldn't fault the man's desire for a more conventional life. "There's always the mines."

Jonas's mouth turned downward at the corners, but he didn't outright refuse. "That is true."

David understood. It wasn't the most appealing option. "The stage company is looking to hire new drivers."

Jonas was even less impressed with that suggestion. "I, ah, think I'd like to stay closer to home."

How could David fault him? A man had to carve out his own future. David's was bent for adventure and opportunity, this man's hope was a bit more...domestic in nature. "I'll keep my eyes and ears open. If I hear of anything, I'll let you know."

"Thanks." Then Jonas offered a genial smile.

The door to the office creaked and the blonde woman exited. Only, it wasn't some random woman...it was Mary Foster.

Her eyes widened as her gaze settled on him. "D-David?"

He tried to smile, but her appearance had taken him by surprise as well. So, he tipped his hat in greeting. "Mary."

Jonas looked between them.

Wait...Jonas had escorted *her* to the telegraph office. Then she had to be the woman he intended to settle down with.

David's heart stuttered. And a sinking sensation filled his gut. Why he should feel so out of place, he didn't know. But he did.

Jonas touched her arm. "Are you well?"

She nodded at him, wrapping a hand around his forearm.

David's gaze caught on the gesture. She seemed to seek support from Jonas. There was definitely more to the interaction than David wanted to acknowledge. His heart burned. How long had this been going on? Were they courting? Or had they come across each other in town as acquaintances?

"What are you doing in Cripple Creek?" Mary said, finding her voice before he did. Even if her words were shaky.

"I have been working with an experienced driver, Hank. We made one last run together before I take my own route."

She bit at her lip. And the silence between them stretched until it strained.

Jonas appeared uneasy. Why should this situation be such? There was nothing untoward between David and Mary. No intention, no deeper feelings.

Then how did David explain his resentment?

"We don't want to keep you," Mary finally said, breaking the thick silence. "Certainly, your family will be eager to see you."

He frowned. Yet another thing he would have to face. Or did he?

"You *are* planning to see them, aren't you?" Mary's entreaty was gentle, but he felt scolded all the same.

"I...am not sure. I have a lot to do before we head out in the morning."

Mary's soft eyes hardened slightly.

He felt the urge to explain. "I...things aren't as easy between us."

Her brow creased as her full lips turned down. "I know that Katie would be devastated if you didn't at least stop by."

He had not really considered that. What if his family got word he had been in town and didn't bother to come see them? They would be insulted. And hurt. Perhaps beyond repair. A cavern of ache opened in his chest. Was there truly any other option? He must face them now or accept that the rift would become a chasm.

Mary stepped toward him, releasing Jonas for the moment. She lowered her voice. "I know it can't be easy. But it is the right thing."

Her wide blue eyes soothed him and something passed between them. Something he had not experienced in her presence. Nor the presence of any woman. What was it? Like the current of the river pulling at him and surrounding him at the same time.

He couldn't speak.

She looked at Jonas, who seemed as concerned as he was confused, and back to David. "Be assured, I will be praying for you."

The sweetness of her consideration both stirred him and settled his trepidation. She would pray for him. He hadn't realized how much he craved that kind of support.

David opened his mouth, but she turned to Jonas and nodded. The young man held out an arm and she used hers to encircle it.

Only then did she look to David again. "It was good to see you." Her words were an odd mixture of firm and wavering.

"And you." He touched his hat brim.

Then he could do nothing but watch Jonas lead her away. Was it his imagination, or did she lean into Jonas more than necessary?

What were her interactions like with the stranger? Did she speak softly and kindly to him? Did she offer to pray for him?

The very thought tightened David's throat. Everything about the swirling emotion within him, giving way to a coming storm, surprised. Did he...have a care for Mary beyond the simple friendship they had always boasted?

If so...if he had been so wrong about the lack of his regard for Mary, what else might his heart be deceiving him about?

He turned in the direction that would lead him to Stoney-brook Ranch. Should he deny his heart's urge for self-preservation and do what was right by his family as Mary suggested? No matter how difficult? And he was once again at a crossroads. Which path would he choose?

Passing Through

David looked at a landscape as familiar as his own face. It had always been home. Had been. Was it still? He didn't know. But he trusted he was about to find out.

He wondered, too, if Ma was in the kitchen working on something. Was Pa in the field? Or maybe in the barn? And Katie would be home from school by now.

But could he face them? He swallowed, that same thickness filling his throat. There was reason to doubt. Was it better to be found wanting? Or the guilt he had lived with these past weeks?

Mary's words came back to him...and the concern in her eyes. She was right. His family deserved for him to face them. How easily Mary once again, for the millionth time since he left town maybe an hour ago, invaded his thoughts. How long had she been courted by Jonas? And why did he have to be such a pleasant fellow? That made it more difficult for David to despise him.

Then again, he didn't know the man. Should David have offered to escort Mary home? Did he err in leaving her with

Jonas? Yes, that was more like it. Maybe he didn't have to hate Jonas, just question his motives.

David grimaced and pushed that to the side. Were his thoughts about Mary because he felt more for her than he'd supposed? Or did they simply serve as a distraction from what was ahead? He glanced once more at the house across the field.

Tempted to turn back toward Cripple Creek, he shifted... and paused. The right thing was obvious. But the easy thing called to him. Well, perhaps easy in this moment. Yet, that decision would likely haunt him for the rest of his days. And would only serve to further alienate him from the family he still loved so dearly.

That is, if that rift torn in his family was even possible to repair. He had injured Pa...unwittingly for the most part. His father's respect for him and his father's plans to pass the ranch to him had both been decimated in moments.

Still, David refused to fault himself for speaking the truth and following his own path.

There was hope in it...for him. But was the price too high?

There was one way to find out. He gathered his courage and urged the rented horse onward down the dirt path. Not wishing to prolong it, nor ready to speed it, he kept the animal at a steady pace. Pushing aside that the closing distance may well signal a loss of his resolve.

Soon enough, however, he stopped the horse just beyond the porch. Mental images of playing with Katie about these wooden boards filled his awareness. And his heart was sad.

Sucking in a breath, he steeled himself for his family's reaction. And hoped Pa would not be in the house. Might he have a chance to see his mother and Katie without that added pressure?

He dropped off the horse just in time to see the front door fly open.

"David!" Ma's voice quaked as she rushed down the few stairs. "Is it really you?"

He clenched his jaw to keep his mouth steady, loosening only enough to speak briefly, "Hello, Ma."

Now off the porch and the steps no longer an obstacle, Ma closed the remaining gap quickly and wrapped her arms about him.

He opened his mouth, but no words came. Just the warmth of her unconditional love and approval. Why had he left this?

She held onto him. "Are you back?"

"For a couple of days," he managed. "I'm coming through Cripple Creek with the stagecoach. Sorry I didn't write or—"

She shook her head as she pulled back. "Never mind with that. You're here! That's all that matters."

His mouth tipped upward. He had missed this more than he had imagined. So much it made him ache all the more.

"Ma, who's—?" Kate stepped out the front door...and halted, her mouth agape and her body frozen. Then she came to life again. "David!" She ran toward him.

Ma barely had time to step out of the way before Katie threw herself into David's embrace. He squeezed her. How had he not realized how much he had missed his troublesome sister? Though she could create drama, they were each other's steady support. No matter what.

"Please tell me you are here to stay." Her words pled more than he'd have liked. They deepened the chasm in his chest.

He frowned. "Just for a couple of days."

She jerked back, a pout turning her bottom lip out.

"Sorry, Katie. I..." What could he say? There were no reassurances he could offer. Not only was it just for the night, the new route he had been assigned would not bring him close to home. That had seemed a good idea at the time, but now he regretted it.

"Never mind that," Ma said. But her eyes glistened, defying the casualness of her tone. "We are thankful for every moment we have with you."

He smiled. As much as he wished her words would ease his burden, they only assuaged it the slightest measure. For he did not know what would happen when Pa came in. And that, he dreaded more than he had any of this.

Ma gripped his arm. "Let's get you inside. You must be tired from your trip."

Indeed he was. Exhausted. The travel had been bumpy, but the strain of the guilt had also taken much out of him. He nodded and allowed her to lead him up the steps and into the home, which smelled strongly of Ma's stew.

His mouth watered, as did his eyes. He hadn't had a well-made meal, much less a homecooked one, since he had left. Far too long to be without Ma's skill in the kitchen.

"You go on upstairs to your room and rest a spell." Ma released him and prodded him toward the stairs.

"I'd rather spend time with you," he protested as he stilled.

Ma's eyes watered even more and she turned away for a moment, feigning a need to check her hair. But he was certain her fingers swiped at her eyes.

Katie grabbed for his arm. "Let's at least have a seat." She pulled him to the dining table. "Did you see the decorations for the Spring Dance?

As a fact, he had not. They may have been set up already in town, but he had not even noticed. He'd been too caught up in his own world. "I didn't know that was tonight."

Katie nodded. "How fortunate to have you home for it. I can think of a few ladies who will be glad as well." She grinned just before slapping a hand over her mouth. "Forgive me my tongue. I shouldn't have said that."

He looked at the tabletop, not wishing her to see evidence of his face heating. And he couldn't help but wonder if one of those ladies happened to be Mary Foster. But he shook his head...that was wishful thinking. She was likely going with Jonas Anderson. Pity.

Pity? Did his mind really just go there? That was wholly ungentlemanly. Still, he couldn't help but mull over his reaction. Would there be a chance to feel it out? Consider what was underneath? As if he didn't know.

"Ma, can David escort me to the dance?" Katie looked across the space and into the kitchen where Ma stirred their dinner.

"I think it might be good if we have David home to spend time with him." Ma set the large spoon down and settled the lid on the pot. Then she turned. "That is, unless you would like to go."

He held his hands up. "That's not necessary. Unless Katie needs me to go with her."

Katie glanced between Ma and David, seemingly unsure of what to say. Then her shoulders slumped. "No...it's fine."

Was Katie hoping to run into Timothy Johnson there? David wondered after that pairing often. Would Timothy be as suited to Katie as she hoped? On the other hand, it was clear that Wyatt Sullivan made overtures, though disguised and a little abrasive. Still, that young man's interest was clear. At least to David. Maybe not to Katie...as veiled as it was.

That was something David did not want—games. When it was time for him to court, he wanted to be clear and ready to embrace the whole of it. But that wouldn't be for some time yet. How could he court a woman if he could barely provide for himself, much less a family?

He sighed. Maybe it was best Mary had been receptive to Jonas. She deserved to be admired, pursued, and appreciated. It would be best if he let this thing go. And why not? It was a fleeting thing, for certain...catching him by surprise. It wouldn't linger.

Then why did he keep thinking about her?

Ma set a glass of tea in front of him with a smile.

He returned her grin and wrapped a hand around the glass before taking a swig. When he set it back down, he noted that Katie watched him. Because she had missed him? Or was there something deeper there?

"What?" The word slipped out of David's mouth before he could stop it.

She jerked a little. "Nothing. Just…"

Why did it seem she searched for words?

"…glad you're home."

There was a hint of disappointment in her voice. Because he wouldn't be taking her to the dance? Or because he couldn't stay?

The door creaked and swung open.

"Lauren," a voice called.

A deep voice. A familiar voice. Pa's voice.

"Whose horse is that outside?"

Mary settled onto the edge of her bed. It was hopeless. She had been trying for the last hour to work her hair into some configuration that would be appropriate for the dance. But she couldn't make her fingers maneuver correctly. They trembled and shook. Because of *him*. She was quite certain of it.

Why? Why did he have to come back to Cripple Creek? And what were the actual odds of them coming across each other as he came through?

She dropped her face into her hands. What was she going to do? Jonas was a nice man. A good man. And she had been receptive to his suit. It wouldn't be fair to reject his overtures at this point. But something in her wondered if it would be fair to allow his feelings for her to deepen given what she still felt for David.

Nothing she had done helped. All the work to put him in the past, to put her care for him to the side...only to have it all crash through the flimsy walls she had erected around her heart.

And once more, she struggled to place how her heart had become so entangled without provocation from him.

Turning her face upward, she sought prayer. But the words wouldn't come. What comfort might she find there? Was God not the source of hope and His will ultimate over her momentary afflictions? Then why couldn't she surrender this?

Wiping at her eyes, she moved to her mirror again. Her hair was partly pulled up and piled on top of her head. But only a portion of it had been tamed. Unruly waves rebelled and refused to be pinned. What a mess.

Footfalls just beyond the door made her heart jump. Was Jonas here to collect her already? She turned toward the barrier as a light knock sounded.

"Yes?" She couldn't escape the dread in her own voice. That was unnecessary.

"Are you ready, dear?" It was Ma.

Mary pushed out a breath. "No."

The latch moved and the door hinges creaked. Ma's features became visible in the small opening.

"Is Jonas waiting?" Mary held her breath.

"He's not here yet. I just wanted to check on you." Ma opened the door wider and slipped in. "What is your plan for your hair?"

Mary peered into the mirror and frowned. "I can't make it do anything."

Ma moved to where Mary sat and reached for her tresses. "Hand me pins as I need them."

Mary nodded.

"And hold still," Ma chided.

"Yes," Mary said, smiling in spite of her trepidation.

Ma tugged and pulled, sometimes a bit harder than Mary preferred. But she continued to maintain her composure as directed.

After several minutes, more than it should have taken, Ma stepped back. "There. Just lovely."

Mary glanced at the mirror. Indeed, Ma had worked a miracle. "It is. I can't believe you managed it."

"I may be older, but I haven't lost my touch. Not yet."

Mary turned to look at her mother's face. The quirk of her smile betrayed that she teased. Still, Mary felt compelled to say, "That is not what I meant."

"Oh, I know, dear." Ma then smoothed over wrinkles in Mary's dress that Mary knew were not there. Not after she had worked so hard to press it. "You are so grown up."

Ma's words tugged at Mary's heart. It wasn't so long ago that Mary needed Ma to do her hair every day for school. But now she was a capable young lady who managed herself. That didn't mean she no longer needed her mother.

Unsure of what to say, but desperate to communicate her heart, Mary wrapped arms around her mother's shoulders.

Ma's tender embrace calmed Mary—about the evening and about her future. God had always taken care of her, blessing her more than she deserved. And He would continue to be faithful, come what may. Of that, she was certain.

A knock on the front door pulled at Mary's attention.

Ma, too, looked that way.

The door opened and Mary heard Pa greet Jonas.

Mary's heart fluttered. Yes, this was right.

Ma reached up and gently pinched at Mary's cheeks. "There now."

Mary gave her mother another quick hug before stepping around her and out into the great room.

Jonas stood just within the house, conversing easily with Pa. But as Mary entered the room, their words dried up. And Jonas's eyes widened.

Pa was the first to find his voice. "Mary, you look...beautiful." Then he looked to Jonas. "Doesn't she?"

Jonas nodded numbly as he stepped farther into the great room and toward her. "I...yes. Just stunning."

Mary was certain her cheeks became even more colored than what Ma had accomplished with her pinching. "Thank you." Her words were shyly delivered. Had she really been reduced to such?

"Jonas, I've hitched the wagon," Pa said as he clapped the man on the shoulder. "I hope you two have a fine evening."

Jonas nodded but didn't take his eyes off Mary. "Thank you, sir."

Pa chuckled and opened the door for them to make their exit.

Mary glanced back at Ma, who had followed her, and smiled once more.

Ma offered a wink as she sidled up to Pa.

Jonas held out an arm for Mary and she slid a hand onto his forearm to let him lead her outside. And tried not to imagine anything else. Least of all what David Matthews would think of her now.

CHAPTER 8

Silence

David watched Pa halt as he stepped inside the home. There was no answer forthcoming from any of them. None was needed. For Pa scanned the room and his gaze stopped on David.

But it did not remain. Pa's features registered an initial shock, then hardened—his jaw clenched and his mouth set firmly into a thin line.

David swallowed. Should he speak into the silence first? Break the tension created by his being here? He wanted to, but no words came to mind and his heart squeezed painfully.

Ma, ever quick to rescue the men in her life, rushed to Pa's side. "Isn't it wonderful? David is home for a couple of days."

Pa's narrowed gaze cut to David again before meeting his wife's. He opened his mouth but closed it again without a sound. He moved to the pump sink in the kitchen and pressed the handle to start the flow of water.

David didn't know what to say. His opportunity had passed. Looking to Ma, he hoped his face didn't scream of his helplessness. Or maybe he did wish her to know.

Ma offered him a small smile, as if encouraging him to

speak into the moment. A slight movement of her hand even directed him so.

"Ma made stew," Katie said. She was never one to be comfortable with long drawn out quiet even in normal conversation. Much less when it was laden with such strain.

Pa quirked the side of his mouth toward his daughter and glanced at the pot on the stovetop. "So she did."

Then the air was thick again with unspoken things. What might David say—or do—to ease it?

He cleared his throat. "I came in this afternoon on the stagecoach. Actually...I drove the stage today."

Pa's stern expression had returned. He muttered something. And David wished he could catch the words. But were they words?

"I...had a little help." David licked his lips, praying for Pa to soften even just a little. "The man I've been riding with, Hank, rode shotgun messenger for me."

Pa grabbed for a dish towel and dried his hands. He all but ignored David. What did Pa expect? David was doing all he could, to the very limits of his courage. Pa had to give...if just a bit. This wasn't fair.

David ran a hand through his hair. "I'm downright eager to have my own route."

Pa stepped to the dish cabinet and swung the small doors open.

"Don't worry about that," Katie pressed as she came up behind Pa. "I'll set the table." She slid in front of Pa and grabbed a stack of bowls.

How could Pa treat him this way? It wasn't right. Sure, he may have made choices Pa didn't like, but they were his to make. Weren't they? And Pa might have missed his help, but it wasn't as if Pa had ever really needed him.

Katie sidestepped a still quiet Pa and waved a hand in

David's direction, a meaningful glance toward Pa. "Why don't you—?"

"Because he doesn't want to." The words were out before David could stop them. "Don't you get it, Katie? He doesn't want to talk to me."

Ma gasped and the steel in Pa's gaze eased for just a second.

Katie set the bowls on the edge of the table.

David pressed on. "Why must I be treated this way for wanting my own life? How long will I be punished?"

"David..." Ma's entreaty was gentle. It didn't matter. For it fell on deaf ears.

Looking at her, David wanted the ability to brush off Pa's behavior, but he couldn't. He was injured by it. So he glared at Ma and challenged, "What sin did I commit? How is it wrong to want my own life?" Never mind that the words were meant for the man who wouldn't speak to him, David directed them at Ma.

Pa gritted his teeth and tossed the towel onto the counter. Would he say something now? It appeared as if he measured his breaths in preparation to do so.

David held his own, straightening his shoulders to stand up against whatever was thrown his way.

Pa's eyes narrowed, then he dropped his regard to the floor.

Were Katie and Ma shaking as much as David? Though David was certain his trembling was from his effort to restrain anger. Wasn't it?

Pa moved past Katie and straight to the back of the house without another word. But they all heard the bedroom door slam.

Ma's eyes were not as gentle when her gaze settled on David this time. She pressed her lips together and followed Pa's retreat.

David gripped the back of a nearby dining chair. Though

he finally breathed, it was as if the air had been knocked out of him. Every inhale was difficult.

A hand touched his arm. He looked at it—Katie's small fingers lay on his forearm—her touch soothed. But he didn't want it. He wanted to nurse his anger. Yet he couldn't make himself shake her off.

He released a ragged exhale.

Katie spoke, her words barely loud enough to discern. "Pa doesn't mean—"

"Yes, he does." David shot a look at her.

She drew her hand back as if stung.

He pushed out another breath and ducked his head. "I'm sorry. It's not your fault."

Another silence fell over the room. But it was pregnant with regret. No matter how much he thought his words had only been meant to defend himself, he couldn't justify the disrespect.

Moments passed, each taking longer than the last.

The stillness was broken by the creak of the bedroom door.

David straightened from his hunched position. Perhaps he should apologize. Not for his words—which he couldn't regret—but for the harshness of them.

But Ma alone appeared in the great room doorway. Her eyes were sorrowful.

David opened his mouth, but his trepidation was too great to allow him to speak.

"Perhaps," Ma said, drawing out her words, "It would be best if you took Katie to the Sweetheart Dance this evening after all."

David jerked back. He felt Katie staring at him. What could he say? Dare he refuse and insist Pa speak to him? He wasn't a child. But rather than fight it, he nodded.

Katie looked between him and Ma. "But—"

A shake of Ma's head silenced Katie.

Moving farther into the room, Ma set a hand on Katie's shoulder. "Why don't you put on the dress we just finished pressing? Then I'll help you do something with your hair." Ma then glanced at David.

Was this an opportunity for him to approach Pa alone? Was that what she suggested?

Her next words cut him off. "David, you should probably hitch the wagon."

Then it was settled—Pa did not wish to speak to him. Perhaps not ever again.

As much as the heaviness of that realization filled David's gut like an anchor, he managed to nod and turn toward the door. Ma did not try to stop him as he took his leave. And, once outside, he leaned against the door's exterior.

What was he to do? He couldn't live under his father's thumb. This was how it had to be, then. So he pushed off the door and swallowed his hurt once again.

Mary drew in a deep draw of mountain air. What could be better than an evening with Jonas? She glanced at his profile as he directed the horse onward. Did he know she stared? Jerking her attention forward again, she hoped to avoid him finding out. He was a fine gentleman—handsome, gentle, attentive. And he cared for her. Wanted to court her. Perhaps even sought to marry her.

That was more than she could say for David Matthews.

She stopped that thought right where it was. Tonight was about spending time with Jonas. She refused to dampen it with thoughts of something that would never be.

"What time was the Sweetheart Dance supposed to start?" Jonas's words slipped through the tension in her muscles.

"Pardon?" Facing him, she saw that his gaze was trained on something in the distance. But what?

"This get together? When was it supposed to start?" He peered at her and frowned. How many times had he asked? Hopefully, just the two.

"Um...five o'clock I think."

"Seems they started a bit early."

What? How could he—?

But as she watched him, he jerked a hand in the direction they were headed. And she caught the sounds of music breaking through the once still night. The banjo and jug cut through the clomp of the horses' hooves even. How had she missed it? Oh yes, she had been lost in thought.

"And here I was concerned we'd be early." Jonas grinned.

She offered a small smile. "That would have been fine."

His brow furrowed. "But now we can make a grand entrance. And everyone will see the prettiest girl in Cripple Creek on my arm."

Her face heated and she laid a hand on his arm. "You are too kind."

He looked at her. She sensed it even though her gaze was settled on the lights now visible in the fast approaching town center.

"I just call it like I see it. You are the prettiest girl in town. Maybe in all of Colorado."

Her blush deepened. She wanted to beseech him to stop, but she couldn't form the words.

"Especially tonight." His voice dropped an octave.

She wanted to meet his gaze, wanted desperately to be able to accept his words. But she felt guilty. For her heart longed for David to speak such words.

What was wrong with her? Could she not put him in her past? Perhaps she had gotten off to a good start with that...

until he showed up today. Their passing had shaken her...and left her doubting her ability to move on.

No. She could. More, she would. Of that, she was determined.

The cart slowed to a halt.

Mary turned to ask Jonas what the matter was only to see him shift and drop from the driver's bench.

Looking about the cart, she realized they had arrived at the General Store. And again she chided herself for being so absorbed in her thoughts.

Jonas walked around the cart and raised his arms to assist her down.

She settled her hands on his shoulders and let him guide her to the ground.

His touch was firm and careful. And held none of the pleasant tingles that ran through her whenever David was near.

She pushed that thought to the side as well. There was nothing for it. Such notions wouldn't lead her anywhere good.

Now she and Jonas stood face to face, a bit closer than usual. His eyes seemed to study her. What did he see? Then, as if remembering something, he released her and backed away a step.

"Shall we?" He held out an elbow for her. Such a gentleman.

She set a hand in the crook of his arm and once again determined that she could move past this.

They didn't speak further as he led her into the area of the main stretch set aside for the gathering. Several couples twirled about as music filled the evening sky.

Laying her other hand atop the one already on his arm, she shifted a little closer.

He stiffened slightly. What was that about?

Perhaps nothing more than her movements taking him by surprise.

"Thank you for escorting me this evening." She softened her tone as she put forth in her words all the good feelings she felt for him.

He glanced at her. "It was my pleasure."

They stood, watching the townsfolk swirl, kicking up dust. For several moments, they did just that.

Jonas tapped his foot to the beat and she made an effort to focus on him—his enjoyment of the cadence, his steady presence.

It was more than David had given her. Though he had been her friend, he had never made any overtures toward her. Nor did he give any indication that he cared. Even more, he had left town the first chance he got. Why would she still hold onto a shred of hope?

Was that what she did—hold onto something, even a shard, of a dream of him? Of her and him?

Pressing closer to Jonas, she wished that his closeness could help her push those thoughts away.

The fight within her continued. But she noted that the music came to an end. That meant the next round would start soon.

She should resist the urge to be bold, but desperate times called for greater measures. So, biting back her trepidation, she said, "Care to dance?"

He looked at her, his face a mask. Was he embarrassed by her forwardness? Ashamed? Then a smile spread across his features. "Of course."

Her rising concern dissipated and she grinned.

He led her to the center of the dance area. The very dead center.

She nodded to the couples they passed, friends she knew well and who now saw her with Jonas. Did they wonder what happened between them? Had Jonas made their courtship public knowledge? That didn't seem like him.

Halting, he tugged her into position in front of him. His eyes gleamed as he set a hand to her waist and the other held hers, neither demanding nor pressing, just holding her.

The first strains of the music sounded and he moved in step with the beat.

She gave herself to the moment. As she spun, she laughed. The movements he guided her through were dizzying, but there was only Jonas and her.

And then there was David.

David? Had her eyes deceived her?

She shifted her focus to the crowd even as Jonas continued to twirl her.

Yes, he was there.

And he was staring at her.

Right. At. Her.

Her feet would no longer obey and she stumbled.

Jonas's grip tightened, but it was too late.

She crumpled into a heap on the ground.

CHAPTER 9

Nearness

How could this have happened? Mary wished she could just disappear. But that wasn't possible. At least not in this nightmare.

Jonas disentangled his limbs and leaned over her.

"Mary, are you all right?" Concern filled his voice.

She nodded even as her face burned. "I am." Glancing around, she prayed she wasn't a spectacle.

Too late.

Jonas's gaze followed hers. Then he looked to her again. "Are you certain?"

"Just...help me up." If only he were able to shield her from all the eyes. Especially two dark brown ones that she could feel on her.

Jonas reached for her, setting hands just under her arms to lift her.

As she rose, she found her footing.

And fell again.

This time, Jonas kept her from dropping to the ground.

"I'm not sure you are well." He gave voice to what she'd rather ignore.

"Can I help?" Another voice joined Jonas's. But she wouldn't look. If her eyes didn't confirm her worst fear, it wouldn't be true, right? Though it was futile. Her head shot around and met David's gaze, worry etched on his features.

"Yes, thank you," Jonas said before she could interject.

David came alongside her, opposite Jonas and helped her hobble to a nearby bench. Jonas released her as David settled her onto the firm surface. Why did his touch have to light a spark within her? And why must her cheeks heat all the more as she tried to disguise her reaction?

Jonas ran a hand through his hair. "I think I should go for the doctor."

Mary jerked her gaze toward him. "No. I will be fine. I just...stumbled."

Jonas didn't appear so certain.

And David interjected, "I think one of us should. Mary, you need to be tended."

She frowned. But as her eyes met David's she couldn't pull away. There was something in his regard...something she hadn't seen before. Or was that her wishful thinking? For certain, after embarrassing herself, there could not be such.

Still, his hand lingered on hers. And sent fire shooting up it.

"I will," Jonas pressed out the words. Was he upset with her? Did he suspect her thoughts about David?

"I'll stay with her." David settled on the bench beside her. Not so near he risked impropriety, but close enough to set her nerves on edge.

She wanted to protest, but Jonas's shrinking back was all that was left of him.

David moved his hand to her shoulder. Did he have to?

Could he feel her skin searing? "Is there anything I can get for you?"

Why did his voice have to be so gentle? So concerned? Why did he have to draw out her more vulnerable feelings— the ones that she had tried time and again this last month to bury? It was as if none of that had been effective, for her tender feelings for him rushed to the surface. Stronger than ever.

She chanced a glance at him.

His eyes were wide and reflected his disquiet.

She pulled her gaze away and focused on the tear in her skirt.

The tear in her skirt? When had that happened?

She wanted to push out a frustrated sigh. Of course it had to have been when she fell. But she hadn't been aware of the cloth ripping.

Pulling at the tattered pieces, she tried to cover the slit that gave others a glimpse of her petticoat. It worked...somewhat.

"Are you uncomfortable?" David asked.

If only that weren't the case. As it were, her discomfort was more about the war within than her injured ankle. "I'm fine."

She looked away, praying Jonas would be quick.

"You have a..." David said, hesitant.

She glanced at him.

He pointed to her hair.

Reaching up, she felt that a comb was out of place and dangling from a lock of hair. Could she just die right here and now?

Tugging at the offending piece, she tried to free it. But it wouldn't budge.

"Let me." His words were softer than necessary.

She opened her mouth to naysay him, but his fingers covered hers and moved through the tangled strands.

He was much closer than she'd prefer. It...stirred something in her. Something she would not give into. Even so, she doubted that determination would hold.

As he worked on the comb, she found she could not turn away. So she quite openly stared at him while his attention was on her hair. Surely, he wouldn't notice.

Then his eyes met hers.

Her breath caught.

His movements paused as his gaze delved into hers.

How could she be so hot and not burst into flames? She told herself to pull back, to turn away...something. But she could no more move than she could stop her heart from beating.

"Mary, I..."

Why were his words so heavy?

Then the comb dropped from his hands.

It disrupted the moment enough that he shifted his focus. Reaching down, he gathered the offending object and held it out to her.

"Thank you." She licked her lips but couldn't make herself look at him again. "And thank you for caring...I mean, for caring enough to wait with me."

A thick silence fell between them. What was he thinking? Dare she look at him to try and gauge it?

After another long moment, she did peer up.

"I do care," he breathed out.

Her eyebrows rose. "What?"

"There she is," Jonas's voice carried from several feet away.

David turned in the direction of the sounds. "Thank goodness you're here, Dr. Shaffer."

Indeed, as she looked, she spotted the older man in tow with Jonas. "Yes, thank goodness."

David moved back, making a space for the doctor. And she immediately regretted his distance.

She shot a look at him, but he wouldn't meet her eyes. It seemed as if his words had meant more than just simple concern for a friend. Was that possible? And more, what was she to do about it?

David noted that the men drawing near moved somewhat slowly. Dr. Shaffer had aged much in the last year. Yet he was still capable of caring for the people of Cripple Creek. But for how long? Not that it mattered...all that David cared about was Dr. Shaffer be able care for Mary. That was of utmost importance at the moment. So much so that it pained him to separate himself from her and give the doctor space to do his work.

Sliding off the bench as he rose, David stepped a couple paces away before he looked back. As much as he wanted to consider Dr. Shaffer's movements, his gaze latched onto Mary.

Did she, too, hate the distance created by him? He shouldn't have let himself get swept up in the heat of the moment. That wasn't right. Had he pushed too hard? That hadn't been his intent.

Studying Mary's face, he noted that her mouth twisted in pain and her eyes held a sadness about them that hadn't been there before. He could make himself believe it was because of the sudden absence of his nearness, but there was little to support such an assumption. Except...did he want her to miss him?

Dr. Shaffer spoke to Mary, but in a tone such that David couldn't make out his words.

Mary nodded and, leaning back against the outer wall of the General Store, moved her leg until it was a good couple of feet off the ground.

She grimaced and let it fall, striking out a hand for support.

David jerked forward as if to answer her beseeching.

But Jonas was there first, taking her hand and settling on the bench. Probably closer than he needed to be. Or so David thought.

Still, it didn't escape David's notice that Mary gripped Jonas's hand so tightly her knuckles paled.

Dr. Shaffer felt along Mary's ankle.

She gasped as he did so and leaned into Jonas.

It was too much. David hated that the sight of her pressing into Jonas was as difficult to watch as the evidence of her pain.

What a cad! He shouldn't have such thoughts. His only mission had been to ensure Mary was cared for and tended to.

Well, now she was. By Dr. Shaffer...and by Jonas.

Was David even needed any longer?

Perhaps not. He'd assisted Jonas when called upon, but now he was in the way. And no matter how much he wished to remain, there was no point in it. Even more, he had no desire to watch Mary's connection to Jonas on display.

So he stepped back several more paces and, turning, moved back into the throngs of townsfolk. What was his problem with this anyway? Jonas and Mary were in some manner of relationship—courting most likely. That was not something he should interfere with. He wasn't that kind of man anyway—injecting himself where he wasn't wanted. Or welcomed.

He'd had plenty of chances, opportunities galore, to seek more than friendship with Mary. Why hadn't he? Had he not cared to? Or had he suppressed any deeper regard for her in his desire to leave Cripple Creek?

It was difficult to see truth in the mired situation.

Though now his feelings were clear, sharp, and painfully obvious. But that was his loss.

Even were she not courting Jonas, it would be too much to ask for her to wait as he found a way to make a home for a family. His future was uncertain, too much so to involve someone as special as Mary. She deserved more. He couldn't even offer hope. Much less promises.

Yes, it was best he put her out of mind.

Searching for his sister, he noticed her across the way, conversing with Timothy Johnson. Even Timothy had a plan to make a way. He would be headed off to seminary soon, as David understood it.

Either way, Katie and Timothy seemed to be enjoying one another's' company. He didn't want to disturb them, so he found a space near enough to watch them, but far enough that he wasn't tempted to eavesdrop. Though as he did so, it wasn't Katie and Timothy he homed in on. No, his gaze was irresistibly drawn back in the direction from which he had come.

Maybe it was fine for him to dream a little. As long as he kept it to himself.

And dream he did.

CHAPTER 10

Concern

Mary seethed as the movement of the wagon jolted her ankle. Though Jonas did his best to restrain the horse's speed and minimize her discomfort. Dr. Shaffer had wrapped it, but that had done little to diminish the pain. Must it hurt so? The regular shaking of the cart reverberated in her wounded leg and sent a streak of pain through her.

She breathed through it, forcing air in and out slowly. And felt eyes upon her. Peering at Jonas, she noted his gaze jerked between her and the horse. He appeared rather concerned. And...regretful? What did he have to regret? He'd been a perfect gentleman the entire evening, even assisted as well as humanly possible after her injury.

Still, she hoped he hadn't suspected that when she had reached for comfort it had been for David. She was thankful Jonas had intercepted her and offered what support he could.

What had she been thinking? Had she lost her hold on her senses? David's closeness and words must have addled her brain. Nothing had changed in that regard. He would be

103

leaving soon for who knew how long? No promises had passed his lips. No assurances. No admissions.

Even had they, what could she do? There was no way to know what the future—his future—held.

Jonas was a more solid choice. He had expressed his interest and care. And even now, he worked to make a life for himself in Cripple Creek.

No, there was nothing for her with David. She'd best put him out of mind.

The cart rattled and white-hot pain seared through her. Crying out, she wondered if the doctor could be certain her ankle wasn't broken.

Jonas's hand covered hers. "We're almost there." His voice was gentle and held a tinge of sadness. Did he wish he could make the ride easier for her? Eliminate her pain? That was kind...and rather thoughtful.

Yes, Jonas was a good man.

She flipped her hand and interwove their fingers.

At first, he pulled back but then settled his palm against hers with a squeeze.

Mary wanted to thank him, or at least assure him she would be fine. But with teeth clamped against groans of discomfiture and expressions of pain, her efforts were cut off. So she made do with what could be communicated through their hands pressed together.

Soon enough, he disentangled himself.

Why? She peered through narrowed eye slits and noted that they approached her parents' homestead. Relief rushed through her...and not only because she would no longer be subjected to this horrid bumping. She could not deny that a part of her wanted to be alone with her thoughts. Mostly, her thoughts of David. Why would that be? So she could dream of something that would never be? Something that would wound Jonas greatly? How would she react if Jonas's thoughts were of another whilst he courted her?

The wagon came to a halt, and she bit her lip to refrain from crying out again.

Jonas stared at her, his eyebrows lifted and mouth downturned. "I'm so sorry, Mary." His address caught in his throat. Was he so shaken by her pain?

She touched his arm. And noticed that her hands trembled.

He rested his hand on hers as his features darkened. "Let's get you inside."

She nodded, though she dreaded what it would take to do so.

He dropped out of the cart and came around. Then, lifting arms for her as before, he issued instructions. "Use your good leg to shift this way. I'll catch you."

Would he? But she knew better. Jonas was someone she could rely on. Someone she could trust to do right by her.

Every pained movement brought her nearer the edge of the seat.

"You're close enough now. Lean down."

She obeyed, stretching a hand to rest on his shoulder.

But when he tugged her down, it was not to assist her in gaining her feet. She landed, somewhat gracelessly, into his arms.

He let out an *oof* as she did so, but his legs held.

Startled by his movement, she gripped him tightly. Now settled, she thanked the Lord they had not ended up in a heap on the ground.

"You all right?" His face was so close.

She couldn't look into his eyes. Not after her wayward thoughts. Instead, she nodded and tucked her face into his shoulder.

He held her securely in his arms and took a few steps forward.

The movement jostled her as well, but not to the same extent as had the cart. Her pain was more of a throbbing in her injured ankle.

Jonas moved slowly toward the front door, pausing at the stairs. Was she too much for him to carry? Was he concerned he might drop her?

But as she pulled back, a question on her lips, she spotted Pa in the doorway.

His wide eyes and arched eyebrows gave away his alarm. How could she explain?

She didn't have to, as it turned out. In this, Jonas rescued her.

"Mr. Foster, Mary has injured her—"

Pa rushed down the stairs, cutting further words off. Had he even heard Jonas?

Mary shifted, perhaps it would be best if they put some space between them, at least what space they could.

But Jonas held her firmly.

She opened her mouth, but Pa reached their position first. His features were wild and his concern palpable.

"Thank the Lord you're home," he pressed out.

This was not the reception she had anticipated. Certainly not with Jonas and her in such a position.

"It's your Ma. Something's wrong."

Ma? Mary wiggled again, attempting to get down.

Jonas grunted and held fast to her.

"Come," Pa managed to sputter.

Jonas followed him up the stairs and into the house. Only then did he carefully settle Mary on her feet, keeping an arm around her for support.

She wanted to shake him off. Her heart raced and panic crept in. What could be upsetting Pa so? It must be serious.

Jonas stayed close, offering his body for support.

When she stepped forward, she nearly cried out. That had been a mistake.

Jonas wasted no time in sweeping her into his arms again.

"This way," Pa insisted, all but ignoring what transpired with his daughter. He disappeared into his and Ma's bedroom.

Jonas followed and Mary feared what they might find. It wasn't until he caught his breath that she realized she was gripping him a bit too tightly.

She relaxed her hold, or tried to.

They slipped through the doorway.

Pa leaned over Ma, who lay moaning.

"Water."

"It's all right," Pa soothed. "Mary's here."

"I'm parched." The words were slow in coming, drawn out and slurred.

"Let me down," Mary said, now pushing against Jonas.

He complied with some hesitation, settling her in a chair near the bed. Had Pa been sitting here, keeping watch?

Jonas leaned toward her again. "Perhaps I should fetch the doctor."

Ma jerked upright. "No! I'm fine, just..." She stared at Jonas as if not seeing him. "Who is that?" Ma said in a harsh whisper that everyone heard.

"It's Jonas. And Mary."

"Oh?" She narrowed her gaze and leaned forward. But not once did recognition dawn on her features. "I'm just a little tired. And thirsty."

Why was Ma behaving so oddly?

"Be a dear and get me some water..."

Mary waited for the remainder of what more she would say, but her words trailed and she didn't speak further.

Ma rubbed her hands together and looked at them, splaying out her fingers.

Pa reached for them as if to stop her strange movements.

She jerked away. "There's an odd…it's like ants are crawling in my fingers."

Mary's breath caught. What had Ma in such a way?

Jonas, too, appeared rather stricken. He glanced about, his gaze catching on something on her nightstand. "What is this?"

Mary craned her neck to see what he had grabbed.

He lifted the elixir bottle to his nose and sniffed. "This is alcohol." His words were grim. Did he think Ma had drunk herself into a stupor? Had she?

"That's the tonic I got for her," Pa said, reaching for it. "It's been helping her."

Jonas trained his gaze on Mary. "I think we need to get her to Dr. Shaffer. And let him see this bottle."

Pa shook his head. "I tell you, it's been helping her. There's nothing to concern Dr. Shaffer with."

"But what if Jonas is right?" Mary blurted. She hated the strained expression on Pa's face when he shifted his focus toward her.

He dipped his head, and nodded slowly.

Mary reached for his hand. "We need to get her to Dr. Shaffer." And as determined as she was to go with them, she did not look forward to more time in the shaking cart. But she hadn't much choice.

"Help me get her to the wagon," Jonas said, setting a hand on Pa's arm. "We'll get her taken care of."

Mary moved to stand.

Jonas halted her with an outstretched hand. "I think you best stay at the house."

"There's no way you're leaving me here."

Jonas seamed his lips and his brow furrowed. He was going to tell her 'no.' If he did, how could she refute him without appearing stubborn?

In the end she decided she didn't care how she seemed to

Jonas. She leveled her gaze and put force into her words. "I'm going."

The townsfolk bustled already and it was only eight o'clock. What else had David expected? Cripple Creek had never been much of a sleepy place, rather busy and overfilled with fortune seekers and miners. Perhaps more than his comfort level would have allowed. Still, he could not begrudge those trying to make their way in the world. Wasn't that, after all, what he wanted for himself?

Turning his attention back to the livery owner, David paid for his rented horse.

The man nodded and pocketed the bills. "Nice to see you back in town."

"Only for a couple of days," David said. Was it necessary to tell the man that? Or was he simply reminding himself?

"If you need another horse, let me know."

"Will do." David shook the man's hand and turned.

But he wouldn't need the horse again. The few waking hours he'd had at home had been altogether unpleasant. He had risen this morning to find that Pa had already gone to the fields. Pa needn't worry, David was not prepared to track him down in the least.

Ma had been unusually quiet at breakfast while Katie had chattered on as if she hadn't noticed. It had been awkward. And he didn't want to put Ma in a position where she drew back into herself. Nor did he wish to create friction between her and Pa. That was not his intention. Never would be.

It was best he just kept a distance. That, too, was not something he needed to share at large. Too many wagging tongues in this town.

He strolled toward the telegraph office. Maybe it would be best all around if he wired a request to leave town sooner.

Strolling beside the General Store, he nodded to passers-by that were unfamiliar to him and greeted briefly those he did know...which, weren't many. As he approached the café, the front door opened, catching him unawares. He halted just short of a woman emerging.

The petite figure and light blonde hair gave him pause.

She jerked around, also startled. And found himself staring into the same light blue eyes that had filled his brief sleep.

His heart thudded. "M-Mary?"

"David." Her widened eyes took him in.

He noticed the crutch under her arm on the same side as her injured ankle. But she seemed to maneuver all right.

"Are you...well?" It was an awkward try, but it was the best he could put forth in the moment.

Her gaze darted to the ground and she licked her lips. Why must his attention latch there?

He forced his focus upward to her eyes.

"I...am," she managed.

He furrowed his brow. She didn't sound confident. Was that because she was somewhat off kilter or because she wasn't truly well? "Are you certain?"

She nodded but trapped her lower lip between her teeth. Was she suppressing more words? Or emotion?

A quick glance back to her eyes told all. Moisture welled there.

He slid a hand to the small of her back and directed her toward a nearby bench.

She resisted for a moment, but soon let him lead her. With great care, she settled and leaned the crutch to the side. Then she gripped her hands together in her lap and watched them.

"Mary?" Concern laced through every fiber of his being.

The sheer magnitude of it overwhelmed him. He wanted to reach out and touch her, but he held back. That wouldn't be right.

"I..." She twisted her mouth as if she warred within herself.

It only intensified his anxiety. And he wondered again if he should have trusted Jonas to get her home safely the night before. A million possible scenarios flooded into his mind. "Please...tell me what's bothering you."

She drew in a ragged breath. "It's Ma."

His pulse calmed at the realization that she was uninjured. Then he came back to himself. "Your ma?"

She nodded, sniffling.

It sent a pang through his heart.

"She has this...condition."

Curiosity reared, but he pressed it down. He wouldn't push her. He would let her share what she would as she was ready.

But he couldn't stop himself from setting a hand over hers. Could he offer her his strength?

"Pa got some of that elixir for her."

Again, David forced his expression to remain neutral and to just listen.

"It seemed to be helping. But Dr. Shaffer says it—" A shudder shook her shoulders.

He touched her arm and offered his handkerchief.

She grabbed for it.

Then he drew back, reminding himself not to push, but to let her take from him as she needed.

"It made things worse."

His eyebrows pinched together. "Made it worse?"

She nodded, blotting her eyes with the white cloth. "It turns out that it's mostly alcohol and little else."

He frowned. While he'd never had need of such a tonic, he'd always suspected it wasn't the cure-all it promised to be.

"And now she…"

He rubbed a thumb across her folded fingers.

"She's not doing well." Finally, Mary glanced at him.

He tilted his head to better meet her gaze. "Does Dr. Shaffer think he can help?"

She looked at their clasped hands. It was as if she was just then noticing. "He doesn't know." Her fingers spread apart as if stretching.

Still, he held onto her hand. "Oh, Mary."

Nodding, she lifted the handkerchief to her face and used it to suppress sobs. Her body shook as she squeezed her eyes shut.

He couldn't hold back any longer. How could any man with a heart? If nothing else, he was her friend, right? Friends cared. And comforted.

Closing what distance was between them, he wrapped an arm around her and drew her to himself.

She fell against him. Surely she was in sore need of the embrace.

Pressing her head to his shoulder, he spoke words that he hoped would soothe. He *prayed* they would soothe.

It wasn't long, however, before he realized where they were. The public display of the moment both shielded her reputation and endangered it. With great reluctance, he drew back.

She didn't question him, but he saw the lingering need in her eyes. If only he could hold her longer. At least until her tears dried and everything was as it should be.

He watched as she tucked errant hair behind her ears. Something that he itched to do. The light touch on her silken hair while he'd held her had been heaven in the midst of the storm. And he was a cad that his thoughts had wandered to such a place. A cad!

Here she needed a friend and he couldn't stop thinking of what it would be like to really embrace her.

"Dr. Shaffer is a good doctor," he finally choked out. "If something can be done, he will know what to do."

She nodded, a hiccup escaping.

The fact that it also endeared her to him made him feel more the heel. What was he thinking?

"Let me walk you back to the clinic." It was the least he could do after he had almost knocked her over and then delayed her return.

She looked down and nodded.

It was as if there were a war within her. Was it possible she still felt for him? That he hadn't missed his chance?

He cleared his throat as he stood. But what could he say that wouldn't sound despicable? No, now was a time to let her be completely focused on her mother. Besides, she was being courted by another man. A man who, from all appearances, was honorable.

Holding out a hand, he helped her to her feet. She leveraged his support as she stood and reached for her crutch. Then, with nothing further, he walked her the few paces to the clinic door.

"I'll leave you here." He had done enough damage.

She reached for the latch but paused.

His heart skipped a beat.

Turning, she offered a small smile. "Thank you. I needed that."

He returned her smile but shoved his hands in his trouser pockets. That was best. Remove the temptation to reach for her.

Then she shifted her attention to the door, opened it, and hobbled within.

His knees became weak. So much so, he leaned against the wall. What was wrong with him? How could this be happening? And what was he going to do?

CHAPTER 11

Interactions

David moved down the planked walkway beside the shops. He didn't know where he was going or what he intended to do once he got there. His heart ached. And he wasn't quite certain how to make it stop.

He hurt for Mary's situation. If he were honest with himself, he would see that he wanted, more than anything, to go back in time. To have noticed. To have responded. To have pursued her. Was it too late?

His shoulder bumped something solid. He thought to keep walking, but turned. Jonas Anderson watched him. Had he rammed into the man? If so, Jonas would be well within his rights to tell David to watch where he was going. But the look on Jonas's face was far from condescending. There was concern. Why?

"Sorry," David mumbled. He owed Jonas more than a simple, muttered apology. Yet he couldn't make more words come.

"No worries." Jonas made no motion to move on.

Would David have to interact with him? This man who held Mary's affection and favor? Surely not. Whether or not

Jonas kept going, it didn't mean that David had to linger. So, he tipped his hat and took a step.

"Wait," Jonas called.

Footfalls from behind warned that Jonas approached. Must he? David pressed out a breath as he shifted to face the man.

Something flashed across Jonas's features. Regret maybe?

"Are you busy? I probably should have asked that first. You seem to be headed somewhere."

A war broke out within David. Should he lie to escape this uncomfortable forthcoming conversation? Or dare he take a risk and let Jonas ask him what he would?

Then it occurred to David...his and Mary's embrace was out in the open. Had Jonas seen it? Now it was David's turn to let regret cross his face, hoping Jonas didn't see it for what it was.

Still, he owed the respectable man a conversation. If nothing more than to clear things up. But what was the truth? So he shook his head. "I'm not busy."

Jonas let out a breath. Relief?

David tried to focus on his words. He would take the man's ire if necessary. After all, if *he* were courting Mary, he wouldn't like finding her in another man's arms. For any reason.

Jonas hesitated, glancing around. Then he spoke. "I...ah... understand that you have been acquainted with Mary for many years."

This was some sort of roundabout way of it. Yet it was Jonas's due. "Yes. We were schoolmates together. Our families have lived in Cripple Creek all our lives."

Jonas's eyes softened, but his features did not relax. "Then you might know her best."

"Best compared to...?" David prodded, letting the question dangle in the air. He felt every bit the coward, but he wasn't prepared to volunteer anything. Did he hope Jonas hadn't seen them?

"Well...me, for one." Jonas rubbed his hands on the sides of his trousers. And he wouldn't look David in the eye. Was he nervous? "She seems...distracted."

David waited while Jonas collected his words.

"I can't tell if it's that she is bored with me. Or maybe disinterested. Have I done something wrong?" The man's gaze shifted as if he were out of sorts.

Should David press that advantage? Hope that Jonas would break the courtship? Or rise above and speak fairly to the man?

"I just..." Jonas licked his lips. This conversation was clearly taking a lot out of him. "I care for her. And I want to do right by her."

What more could anyone ask for? A shard of guilt penetrated David's heart. He let out a ragged breath. "Mary is more...timid than most ladies. And she is rather caught up in what's going on with her mother. I wouldn't read too much into that. She may be distant right now, but she is loyal to a fault."

Everything he said was true. Perhaps *he* was the one reading into his interactions with Mary more than he ought. She was devastated by her mother's condition. And she had agreed to Jonas's court. That was no little thing.

Jonas released a long breath and his shoulders relaxed. "That's true."

David smacked Jonas's shoulder. "Yeah. Just give her a little time."

"Thanks." Jonas seemed to transform into a different person—more assured, more confident. "You're a good friend."

David withdrew his hand and almost cringed at Jonas's words. Had he been a good friend? As much as he wished he had made an overture toward Mary before, he couldn't fault Jonas. In fact, in another set of circumstances, he could see Jonas as a friend.

But not now. Not when he stood in the way of David's heart's longing.

Mary watched as Dr. Shaffer leaned back in his chair. Upstairs, Pa tended Ma. While she wasn't much improved, she wasn't worse either. Mary decided to take the good as it came. A few hours ago, she'd feared the worst. But from all indications thus far, Dr. Shaffer reported best hopes for recovery.

As much as she would recover, that is. For the reality was that Ma would never be cured of this ailment. Any improvement perceived while on the tonic had been deceptive.

"When can we take her home?" Mary pressed into the moment, despite her desire to curl into herself.

"Perhaps in a day or so. I'd like to monitor her for that time and watch her food intake."

Did the doctor not think Mary was capable of managing Ma's diet? Ma had made great strides. In fact, even according to Dr. Shaffer, her improvement from days past was due to the change in her eating habits.

"Mr. Foster is welcome to stay as long as he'd like, but I'd prefer no other distractions." He cast a meaningful glance.

He meant her. He meant that she needed to minimize her time here.

But what was the sense in that? Without Pa's help, could she return home?

She opened her mouth to say such but shut it, reminding herself that it was not the doctor's problem. It was hers. And she would have to make arrangements. "May I speak with my father?"

He frowned. Did he truly not have even a small care for her predicament? At length, he nodded with some reluctance but did not make a move to accommodate her.

She shifted to rise, but Dr. Shaffer pushed out a breath and stood. "I will fetch him."

It was as if he merely pandered to her. She had never known the man to be so stand-offish. Though she would never have described him as particularly caring either. He was competent and did his job. That's what the town needed.

Although in this moment, she wanted for a little compassion.

He stepped around the desk and crossed to the stairs.

She didn't turn, but knew he had started up when she heard the creaking of the first steps.

Now alone, she wrapped her arms around herself. And the memory of David's embrace came unbidden. It had been so comforting, so needed, so...wonderful. She only tarried in that blissful moment for a few minutes, however, before thoughts of Jonas pressed in.

Was it appropriate for her to lose herself in David's platonic gesture when she had made a commitment to Jonas? She needn't wonder. She knew the answer. It wasn't.

Yet she couldn't deny her reaction to David's nearness, nor the depth of her consideration for him. She may have agreed to Jonas's courting her, but that didn't mean it was so simple to leave the hope of David in the past. She had thought it would be. But it wasn't. His return and his attentions had been unexpected. Had he always felt for her? Or was she reading into naught but a friendly concern?

She released a long breath. Either way, there was little conscience in allowing Jonas to pursue her while she felt such for David. It just wasn't fair. And she would have to put an end to it.

That realization did not come gently. A swell of regret

filled her. Could she put Jonas off only to discover that David didn't feel such for her? Would she then be destined to be alone? A spinster? Though in truth she was already a couple years beyond the age at which most women married. At that prospect an overwhelming dread filled her. How could she face such a desolate future? Would she always dream of what could have been?

Still, that didn't mean that she could string Jonas along. She had to do what was right by him.

Blowing out another pent up breath, she resigned herself. Yes, honesty was best.

Two sets of footfalls echoed on the stairs.

She ran her hands along her skirt, straightening out random creases. Would she find herself in the boarding house tonight? Would Pa escort her home?

The men stepped into the room, still conversing quietly.

Pa cleared his throat. "Mary, Dr. Shaffer has agreed to let you stay in one of the recovery rooms. But he—and I—agree that it would be best you don't linger in your mother's room. She needs her rest."

Mary nodded, somewhat stunned by her father's ability to change the doctor's thoughts on the matter. "Yes, Pa."

"There now." Pa turned to Dr. Shaffer and gave a curt nod. "I will make my way back upstairs."

What was she supposed to do?

Pa halted and looked over his shoulder. "Might you check the post, Mary?" Had Pa read her thoughts so easily?

"Yes, Pa." She rose as he continued up the stairs.

Dr. Shaffer settled into his chair and opened one of the books on his desk, all but dismissing her.

And just like that, Mary was out of place. Not needed. Not wanted. It caused a sinking feeling in her gut. Was she truly just in the way?

Hobbling to the door, she managed to slip out into the

main stretch of Cripple Creek. Her eyes stung, but she would not give into her errant emotions again. This was not the time, nor the place.

A figure turned a corner and halted. "Mary?"

She glanced up. "Jonas."

"I've been looking for you." He stepped closer and his gaze warmed. "How are you today? How is the ankle?"

She looked down and then back up. "As well as can be expected."

His gaze settled on the door behind her and his features fell. "And your mother?"

She sighed. "She is strong. Dr. Shaffer believes she will recover."

He let out a breath. "That is good news."

Mary nodded, chewing on her lip. "I suppose."

His eyes seemed to scan her then. "Might I escort you somewhere? Have you had lunch?"

"I have. Just a bit ago."

"Oh." His features deflated.

"But I am free for supper." She forced a lightness into her voice.

"Ah. Well, then, we shall make a plan."

She worked the corners of her mouth into what she thought was a smile. Then she turned her gaze toward the telegraph office. "I'm on my way now to…"

Her words trailed as she spotted David emerging from the small building. Almost as if he sensed her eyes on him, he looked at her. His gentle smile warmed her heart.

She tore her regard away and toward Jonas, who appeared rather confused.

"Sorry," she pushed out the apology as she glanced at the ground. "I am on my way to the telegraph office."

His mouth became a thin line. "Would you like company? Or assistance?"

She shook her head. "I thank you, but I can manage." A quick look back in that direction left her frowning. David was nowhere to be seen. Where had he gone?

Ah, it was likely for the best.

"Where shall I collect you for supper?" Jonas's question broke into her thoughts.

"I can meet you at the café perhaps?"

His brow furrowed.

"I am not sure where I will be later." She hoped that didn't come across as much of a lame excuse as it seemed.

"Very well." Jonas seemed hesitant, but said, "Six o'clock?"

She nodded. "Very well."

They stood in awkward silence. Should she turn and make her way first? Or wait for him to move off? As the moment expanded, and with it the tension between them, she offered a weak smile and stepped down the boarded walkway.

If only she didn't feel so guilty. How to soothe her conscience?

Tonight. She would tell him tonight.

CHAPTER 12

Struggles

Mary had long since tired of struggling to get around. And had become worn out with finding things to entertain herself so she wasn't under Dr. Shaffer's feet nor bearing the weight of that piercing stare. She wasn't wanted at the clinic.

But now, she made her way to the café. Jonas was most likely already waiting.

Jonas.

She had spent much of the afternoon trying to decide what to say and how to say it. It wouldn't be easy, that much she knew. But that didn't mean she shouldn't. That's what courage was, right? Moving forward even when one was terrified.

Mary chided herself for being dramatic. 'Terrified' was quite the word. It didn't fit. She was nervous, yes, uneasy even. But not terrified.

She would simply tell him that her feelings were not what they needed to be for their courtship to continue. That was that. And there was no sense getting worked up about his reaction. It could go any number of ways.

Though she trusted that Jonas would be ever the gentleman—understanding even if hurt. Only...she wasn't certain she deserved that.

She neared the café, hobbling along, her focus on every step lest she topple. But as she glanced up, she spotted him there by the door.

As soon as Jonas turned in her direction, he stretched out long legs and maneuvered to her. Taking her arm, he once again offered his strength to steady her.

"Thank you." Her words were soft. And once more she wondered at the wisdom of her plan. Jonas was reliable, loyal, and kind. What more could she want?

She shook her head. The fact remained that it wouldn't be fair to him to push on. Sure she had developed a camaraderie with him...and maybe that could sustain a decent marriage. But not for her. Not when her heart had such longing for someone else.

"Are you all right?" Jonas's question surprised, though it probably shouldn't.

"I am. Perhaps a little tired."

Jonas halted, catching her a bit off guard.

Mary peered up at him. His features were twisted into a concerned expression. There was something deeper in his regard. What, she could not quite place.

"I should walk you back to the clinic. We don't have to do this." Jonas's words seemed hesitant.

"No, it's fine." She set a hand to his arm. As much as she wanted a real excuse to delay, there was little point in it. "I have to eat anyway."

He watched her for a moment, then said, "I guess that's true."

"Shall we then?" Mary motioned toward the door.

"Ah...yes." He picked up step again, assisting her into the eatery.

Mrs. Abby greeted them. "How are you this evening?"

It seemed as if she would continue, but Jonas cut her off. "Two, please."

Mary glanced at him again. It was unlike him to interject so. As she studied him, she noted a hint of perspiration about his forehead. Perhaps nothing more than having been out in the sun. But his palms were sweaty too. Was he nervous about something?

Mrs. Abby indicated they should follow and led them to a nearby table rather in the middle of everything.

Mary wanted to thank her for being so thoughtful and not making them traverse the whole of the dining area. But didn't necessarily wish to be on display. Still, she nodded at the woman as Jonas pulled out her chair.

Mrs. Abby returned the gesture, waiting until they were both settled before continuing. "Meatloaf and chili are our specials today."

Mary's mouth watered. Mrs. Abby's cornbread and chili were quite the tasty combination.

Jonas spoke up before she could. "I'll have the meatloaf. Mary?"

Beaming at the woman, Mary said, "Chili. But only if I can get two pieces of cornbread."

Mrs. Abby winked. "I'll see what I can do." Her focus shifted to the front door where another couple waited. She muttered a quick, "Coming right up." And then she was gone.

Mary fiddled with the plate and silverware, not sure why she avoided Jonas's gaze. She knew what needed to happen and was determined to see it through. But need it be so soon after sitting? Perhaps such a conversation was best over dessert. At least, that's what she told herself.

So she lifted her head to find Jonas distracted by something beyond the nearby window. She followed the direction of his gaze and couldn't find anything she would pin his attention to.

After some moments of silence, she leaned forward. "Jonas?"

He startled as if he had forgotten she was there.

Now it was her turn to be concerned. "Are you all right?"

"I...yes." His words were again hesitant.

Might she push for more? If she wasn't prepared to break off the courtship, she might pat his hand. He looked as if he needed some reassurance. But for what?

Maybe there was no avoiding the issue. Not even for the time it would take to eat their dinner. "You don't seem all right."

He glanced at his hands, they had balled into fists and were pressed together.

She became all the more worried. "Jonas?"

"I...ah...told myself I would wait," he said, finally meeting her gaze. "But I don't think it can."

Her brow furrowed. What was he after? The nerves, the hesitation, and his demeanor...all spoke to some sort of announcement. Or overture...

He wouldn't.

"Mary, you and I don't know each other well, but I have come to care for you very much."

Oh no. He would.

"Jonas," she said, holding out a hand to halt him. "I need to say something—"

He shook his head. "Let me get this out, please."

She quieted, but her hand fell to the napkin by her plate and she grasped it tightly. Could she really break his heart if he proposed? "But I—"

He cut her off. "Mary, I can't continue like this."

Oh goodness. Not quite what she'd imagined. His delivery

was more clumsy than romantic. She bit her lip to keep from interrupting again.

"I'm sorry. I truly am, but I've tried to get past it. Tried to ignore it or tell myself that it's not what it seems. But I can't." He stared into her eyes. "I can't play second fiddle. Not for as long as we both shall live. I won't."

Wait, what? She blinked. He wasn't proposing. He was breaking things off.

"The last thing I want to do is hurt you, but I just can't..." He fumbled and seemed to hunt for more words.

She reached across the table and laid a hand on his arm. "You haven't."

His eyes widened. "What?"

She sighed. "You haven't hurt me. The truth is...I don't blame you."

He blinked but didn't speak further.

"You're not...wrong. I do have a care for someone else."

He nodded, swallowing hard. Had he seen something pass between her and David? What was it that made him suspect?

She shook her head, it didn't matter. "And I understand. I don't want to hold you back. It wouldn't be right."

His shoulders eased, and he visibly relaxed.

"I release you from your word. Completely."

Air rushed out of him and he leaned back.

Why the relief? Was it because she wasn't wounded by his decision or that there would be no repercussions of his breaking their understanding? Again, it didn't matter. But she guessed his reaction was due to a bit of both.

"You don't know how I've struggled." He met her gaze again.

She offered a smile. "So have I. You are a good man. An honorable man. And you deserve someone who will be completely smitten with you."

He nodded. "As do you."

She shrugged. "Maybe that will happen one day."

He looked confused. "Do you and David...?"

"No." She drew her hand back. "Though you are right, I have a care for him, there is no understanding between us. I had not ever thought he would give me a second glance."

Jonas seamed his lips.

She released a breath. "Maybe in time I can move past it, but that day is not today."

He quirked an eyebrow. "I wouldn't be so certain. My hesitation is not only due to how I have noticed you regard him. But also in how he watches you. There is more in his manner than friendliness."

She looked away. Dare she put stock in Jonas's words? Only to be disappointed when David left again for the stage-coach route and his grand dreams?

Jonas took her hand. "Trust me."

She returned his gesture with a squeeze. "That is another worry for another day."

Mrs. Abby moved toward their table with dishes of food.

"For now," Mary said, smiling, "I think the only problem will be keeping you away from my cornbread."

He released her hand and pulled his arm back just before Mrs. Abby set the steaming plate down. Soon enough, Mary's chili and cornbread was placed in front of her as well.

"Shall we?"

Jonas grabbed for his fork. "Absolutely!"

David had meandered around the center of Cripple Creek for long enough. But he would be leaving again in the morning and wanted to enjoy it. He had no way of knowing how long it would be before he returned. Part of it was definitely a desire to avoid his father. And...part of it lay in a hope he would cross paths with Mary again.

That was nonsense, though. Had the situation not been clear enough? She was not available.

His heart sank a little more every time he had this conversation with himself. But it didn't seem to matter—he kept hoping. And kept walking.

If he were a praying man, he would visit the church and ask that the Lord to give him direction. But God had never been much more to him than something everyone did on Sunday. Oh, Ma and Pa were devoted, though he wouldn't consider himself to be. While he may agree that God knew best, he also believed God would help those who helped themselves. So be it...that's what he was doing.

Yet as he thought on his departure the next day, it was with more than a hint of sadness. Cripple Creek had changed since the gold rush. But it was home.

He neared the General Store and had to dodge Mr. Yerby's broom. The man swept the planked sidewalk, perhaps in preparation to close for the day. It was strange, David would have thought the man would be needed at home for supper before now.

"You still in town?" Mr. Yerby looked over the rims of his spectacles. "I'd have thought you'd be gone by now."

David forced a smile. "I did some asking and secured a few days in town. I'll be headed out tomorrow."

"Well, it's been nice seeing you. I bet your parents have been downright thrilled to have you home."

David nodded but didn't give voice to his lie. "It's good to be back...even for a short time." And he knew he had meant it.

Mr. Yerby set the broom just inside his store and reached for the door. "I guess I'll see you next time you come through." He waved and stepped within, closing the door and locking it. Then he flipped the sign to its CLOSED position and moved out of sight.

David sighed. Was he truly missed? Or just remembered when he was right in front of someone?

At least Mary seemed to have missed him.

Drat! His thoughts had gotten away from him again. Time to turn them to something more productive. Continuing on toward the boarding house, he passed the bench he and Mary had sat on earlier in the day. He paused and let the memory of her, secured in his embrace, wash over him. That moment had been bittersweet. He hated her pain, but had so loved the feel of her. It had seemed right and fitting for her to be in his arms.

That must be his imagination, though. His thoughts playing tricks on him.

He turned from the bench. And who should be exiting the café at that time? Of course it was Mary—as if he had conjured her with his wishing. She was not, however, alone. Jonas walked alongside her, with her hand resting on his.

David looked down. Would they pass him by? Maybe they wouldn't see him.

No such luck.

Jonas jerked his head in greeting. "David? Is that you?"

David came to life, lifting his regard from the ground. Though he was unable to keep his eyes from soaking in Mary.

He was certain her face reddened. From his staring? What a desperate, loathsome man he had become.

"Jonas, Mary, taking an evening stroll?" David wanted to kick himself. It couldn't be more obvious that they had just finished supper. Out for a stroll? With her wounded ankle? Hardly.

Jonas cocked his head as if curious, but said, "We enjoyed Mrs. Abby's food and company. Perhaps a little too much." As if to emphasize his point, he rubbed his stomach. And yawned.

"A little late for you?" David didn't mean to draw attention to Jonas's rude gesture. But he couldn't help himself.

"It is. I was up early talking with the foreman at the mine."

"The mine?" David wasn't sure he'd heard correctly.

Mary jerked around to face Jonas, an equally curious look on her features.

"I was, um, looking for a job," Jonas said in no uncertain terms.

Mary didn't appear any less disturbed by his explanation. In fact, guilt washed over her. But why?

"I thought you came out here seeking gold." David couldn't help his interjection.

Jonas set his jaw. "I did. But prospecting isn't serving me so well. I wanted some great adventure, but it's honestly turned out to be pretty hollow—bouncing from place to place, no roots to speak of. Besides, I like it here. If I plan to have a home and family, I have to do something more stable."

Was that it? Had Jonas made such an overture to Mary tonight? Had he...proposed? "I see." David hoped his words didn't come across as dejected as his spirit felt.

Silence befell the small group.

Jonas yawned again. This time more pronounced, almost exaggerated. Then he shook his head. "My goodness, I am more worn than I had thought. David, would you mind seeing Mary back to the clinic for me?"

Walk Mary back? That was an odd question. Why wouldn't Jonas escort his future bride?

David noticed that Mary tossed Jonas a pleading look. Did she not even want to spend a few minutes with him?

He opened his mouth to reject the notion, but before he could, he thought better of it. Jonas was not one to shirk his duty. If he asked David to escort Mary, it was because he didn't feel he could. Did he think he would be so distracted that she might become injured?

It was decided, then. So David stepped forward. "Certainly."

"Thank you." Jonas untangled his arm from Mary's and moved aside for David to take his place.

Her expression still shone disbelief and some amount of anxiety.

David took care with offering his arm. Did she think he would behave inappropriately? That he wasn't to be trusted? He wasn't an animal. He could keep his hands to himself. Well, except for a forearm intended solely to assist.

Jonas lowered his head and spoke to Mary. "I shall see you soon." And then he turned and walked off.

David's ire swelled. The man was an enigma. David would never trust someone else when he had a duty to fulfill. Jonas had always seemed a gentleman. Was this a different side of him?

Mary gripped David's arm and took a breath. Perhaps to steel herself from the work of hobbling along.

He needed to focus on Mary now. No matter how it created a war within. Glancing at her, he noted that her cheeks had colored even more and her eyes were set on something in the distance. What started as a brief glimpse of the woman beside him became more. He savored her features, her movements, everything.

"How was the chili?" he couldn't help but ask.

She jerked toward him. "Pardon?"

"Mrs. Abby's chili. How was it?"

She looked in the direction of the café and then at him. "How did you...know?"

He reached out and touched the side of her mouth. "You have a small piece of cornbread here."

Her hand flew to the place he indicated, but he had

already rid her fine features of the wayward particle and so her hand landed on his.

That had been a mistake. The second their fingers collided, there was a current—like that of a strong river—pulling him to let his touch linger.

Her eyes found his and her breath caught. Then she tugged her hand away and spoke. "And that means chili?"

"For you, it does. You can never turn down her chili when cornbread is at stake." A laugh bubbled up and he released it.

Her mouth quirked, and she gazed at her boots. "I am surprised you noticed."

Was she? Just because he had been blind to her in a romantic way didn't mean he had not picked up on certain things about her. Had he always watched her so? Maybe he had always cared and just hadn't recognized it for what it was.

She looked down the walkway in the direction of the clinic. Only then did he realize they had paused. So he picked up his step once more.

A breeze flowed over them in the quiet moment. It was refreshing and served to cool his heated skin.

He couldn't stand the silence. It made the air between them seem all the more thick. "How is your mother?"

"She is recovering. I pray it will be quickly and completely."

"Of course." What else could he say?

Mary nodded and then leaned into him a little more.

"You all right?"

"Just tired. It's been a long day."

For certain, with her situation, it had been. "We're almost there." His words were meant to reassure, but instead they marked his final moments with her. And his heart ached for it. But he would not stop being her friend. Would not stop caring. So, he pressed into the difficult subject. "I am...glad... you have Jonas."

She made a sound as if she cleared her throat.

He waited for her to speak, but she didn't. "He's got a good head on his shoulders. And a good plan." How could he go on? But he needed to...as much for his own reassurance as hers. "He will make a fine husband."

Mary stopped. The movement jerked on his arm and he halted.

He turned to face her. What was that about?

"David," she started, measuring her words. "Jonas and I are no longer courting."

Was this how she would tell him they were engaged?

"Perhaps, then, congratulations are in—"

"Jonas and I are not engaged either." Now she sounded exasperated. "We parted ways."

It took a moment for her words to penetrate his brain and reroute his train of thought. He swallowed. How could Jonas put her aside? "I'm sorry. I...know it may seem difficult now, but perhaps it is for the best."

Her eyebrows furrowed. "You think he ended it?"

There was suddenly a lump in his throat. "Did he not?"

"No." Mary's fingers were trembling, but her voice belied a confidence he wasn't sure he had seen in her. She released his arm. "Well, perhaps it was mutual."

That did nothing for his confusion.

"You see..." Her words softened and she licked her lips. "I cannot continue to let a man pay me court when I have feelings for someone else."

His whole body stiffened. Did she mean him? Or someone else? Had Mary formed an attachment elsewhere?

She gazed up at him, her eyes wide and trusting even as they brimmed with moisture.

Still, he didn't know what to say. Dare he assume something that wasn't meant? But dare he give her the opportunity to escape his regard for her again?

"I..." he said, then cleared a parched throat. "I think that probably is for the best then."

Her pupils covered much of the blue in her eyes. It was as if he could fall into their depths.

He looked down, searching for the right words. He didn't think he could bear it if she meant someone else. "Mary," he said, pressing into the opportunity her silence afforded him. "I need to tell you something. I...have been so wrong...for so long. Years. I have suspected you had a care for me beyond the simple friendship we shared. And I never thought much of it."

Her eyebrows lifted.

Now fully facing her, his hands encased hers. "Until now."

She gasped.

"I think I always have thought more of you than what seemed on the surface." His chest tightened. What if, after all this, she spoke someone else's name?

"Good." The word was so gentle it was almost imperceptible. The corners of her mouth tipped upward. Was she teasing him? "Because I do care for you. So much."

He drew in a ragged breath. "Truly?"

She nodded.

He enveloped her in his embrace, pulling her as close as he dared.

"I always have," she said. "Always."

He pulled back. He had to see her face, had to look in her eyes and see the truth there. Indeed, the swirling emotions proved the veracity of her statement...and her feelings.

He wanted to shout from the rooftop. He never knew that this kind of fullness in his heart was possible.

"Mary," he whispered as he lowered his head, prepared to seal their declarations the best way he knew how.

"Miss Foster?" a voice called from farther away.

David glanced over her shoulder and saw the boy who worked at the livery rushing toward them at a clipped pace.

The youngster slowed as he approached.

"What's the matter?" David asked the out of breath lad.

"Dr. Shaffer, sir. He's looking for Miss Foster."

She spun, nearly collapsing on her injured leg, but David braced her. "Has something happened to my mother?"

The boy shook his head as he tried to pull in air.

"Thank the Lord!" Mary's body went lax in David's arms.

"It's your Pa."

Mary's knees buckled. But David's arms surrounded her and kept her from collapsing into a heap.

What had happened to Pa? Was he hurt? In danger? These things flashed through her mind, each situation she conjured was worse than the last.

She sucked in a needed breath and tried to regain her footing. David's support was wonderful, but she wanted to be braver than this...wanted him to know she was stronger than this.

"We don't know anything yet." His warm voice attempted to reassure her.

He was right—it could be any number of things.

She glanced at the lad.

His eyes were wide—from surprise at her response? Or did he know something he wasn't saying? And, if so, what did he hold back?

"What is it?" She almost launched herself at the youngster, but David's arms held her back. As if he had sensed her desire to lash out.

"I...I don't know, miss. Honest," he sputtered as he stepped back. "Doc Shaffer only said you were needed."

She shifted her gaze toward the clinic. Then, disentangling herself from David, she pressed on. And pain shot up her right leg.

"Careful," David admonished, by her side once again. He settled her crutch under her arm.

Now more stable, she moved with a speed that surprised even her. Though it was not without pain. Still, she pushed through. She had to get to Pa.

As she and David neared the clinic, he rushed ahead and opened the door.

When she caught up, Dr. Shaffer was already in the doorway.

"Where were you?" His words were harsh but not accusing. It didn't stop them from stabbing her with guilt.

"I...I had gone to dinner."

Dr. Shaffer glanced at David. "I see."

She wanted to defend David—and herself—or at the very least clear up the doctor's misunderstanding. But she shoved those thoughts to the side. Assuaging Dr. Shaffer's sensibilities wouldn't change Pa's situation...whatever it was.

"Where is my father?" She stepped closer, hoping the doctor would move.

Instead, he took a step forward, closing the door behind himself, shutting them out of the clinic. He set a hand to her forearm. "I think you need to sit."

Sit? Why would she need to sit? Had something terrible happened? Was Pa in a bad way?

"No," she said as she shook off the doctor's touch.

David's hands, warm and firm, gripped her shoulders. "I think it best." His voice lacked the comfort it had just before. But as he pressed closer, an arm about her, she was more inclined to listen.

Nodding, she let David lead her to the nearby bench. Her heart thundered in her ears. Would she be able to calm down enough to hear the doctor's explanation?

She sat, with David supporting her. Her movements—and his—were a blur. Still, she had taken the doctor's direction and she now glared at him again. "Please...tell me...where is my father?"

There was an undeniable shakiness in her voice. Even she heard it. As if her heart suspected what her mind would not.

"Your Pa..." Dr. Shaffer scratched his head. "He was with your ma most of the afternoon, then he stumbled down the stairs rather unwell. He was confused and his speech was slurred. Seems he...had a severe attack of apoplexy."

Mary stared at him. What was he saying? Apoplexy? Was Pa ill then? Or...paralyzed? She pulled in a breath. "Where is he?"

The doctor frowned.

No. It couldn't be.

David drew her closer.

She pushed against him. The words filled her throat faster than she could weigh them. But she had to know. "Where is my father?"

The forceful words, though tense with emotion, did not seem to faze the doctor.

"I did everything I could, Miss Foster."

She clenched her teeth and again tried to shake free of David. "Where is he?" The words were more cried than shouted, though both filled her voice.

Dr. Shaffer looked down, then met her gaze. "He is gone."

"No!" she screamed as she folded in half. Her world shattered, the pieces lay around her. To such an extent that no one could possibly put the shards back in place. No one.

Everything became dark and she was falling.

Strong arms came around her, holding her together somehow.

She became aware that she knelt on the planked walkway. David hovered over and around her. Why didn't that make this better? But she knew...nothing could. Nothing would ever be right again.

Wailing, she spent her energy on the hurt filling her. "My father," she managed to speak into the world. A world that was now a much harsher place.

"I know," David soothed. "I know." Was that a thickness in his voice?

"He's my *father*," she cried, her hands pressed to her face. The pain encased her from within, filled every crevice of her being until there was nothing left but an open wound.

How long she crouched there, lost in herself, she did not know. But as she spent all the moisture in her body, she looked up.

Dr. Shaffer had left, but David had stayed by her side through all of it.

"I...I need to see my mother." Her throat was hoarse, her words weakened. She looked to David. "Will you take me to her?"

His jaw muscles worked. What was his hesitation? But he then nodded. "Of course."

Mary allowed him to help her stand. There was no more pretense of strength about her. She was broken...and empty. And fearful of what the next day might reveal.

David hung his head. The day was as gray and solemn as they came. Clouds overhead blocked the sun and it had drizzled throughout the day, with promises of more rain to come. Fitting, it seemed, for the day they would lay Mr. Foster to rest. David peered across the crowd at Mary. How he wished he could hold her hand for this dreadfully hard thing. But they were not officially courting. It would not be appropriate for him to be by her side. Still, he longed to be.

She was forlorn. More than that, she was deeply sorrowful. As anyone would expect.

Something else caused his gut to twist—his proximity to his own father, the irony of which was not lost on him.

He and Pa had not exchanged words for a week. And it ate at him. All the more with the realization that anything could happen at any time to anyone. No one had suspected Mr. Foster's time would come to a close. When would Pa's days end? Maybe there was enough reason in it to humble himself and approach his father. But did he have the courage?

Reverend Jones said a few final words and stepped to Mary. He pressed her arm and stood beside her as the towns-folk gathered to pay their final respects.

David could only watch as many spoke soft words of comfort and mourning to Mary before walking off. They had that privilege. Whereas Mary would be left in a dreary place for many days, weeks, or months to come. Would she ever be the same?

Mrs. Foster had not been well enough to come to the graveside. And from her reaction when Mary shared the news with her, David wasn't certain she was completely cogent. A murmur and shake of her head was all they got. Which only served to intensify Mary's grief. Would her ma follow her pa into the afterlife soon?

Unwilling to leave Mary during such a time, David had wired the stagecoach company. It just wasn't possible for him to take on his route. Not yet. But the response he'd received was not as he'd hoped. If he couldn't report for his route, they would have to replace him. He knew what that meant—he would no longer have a job.

It was a sacrifice he had to make. For her.

He watched his parents and Katie moving closer to Mary in the line of those offering their condolences. Did all the faces and words blur together at some point?

Pausing to create a gap between himself and Pa, he waited until the line had completely formed and he stepped to the end. He did not wish to be rushed—or have an audience—for his words to Mary.

And so he waited, with as much patience as he could muster. Though eager to speak with Mary, facing her in her grief had become difficult. Especially with his own challenges in his relationship with his father.

He studied Pa as his parents spoke with Mary, watched as Katie embraced her friend, and saw Mary cling to Katie. Swallowing against rising emotion, he pushed his own problems to the side and focused on the woman he cared for so deeply.

When at last he was alone with Mary and the reverend, he took her hands. And found himself without words.

She offered a small smile and gripped his fingers. "Thank you. For everything."

He nodded. Should he tell her that he now had no plans to leave town...and no reason to? Would that soothe? In the end, he decided that this day was about her father. Not about him. So he squeezed her hands once more and looked after the departing townsfolk.

The reverend had stepped away, speaking with Mr. Hammond. That man, too, had a gaping hole left with Mr. Foster's death...but one more of an annoying vacancy in his staffing than one of loss.

David took the opportunity to lean in and, softening his voice, said, "I'll be by later today to check on you."

She nodded, looking wistfully into the distance.

"Do you need anything?" His heart ached for her. So much.

She shook her head and her eyes misted. From all she had poured out in his presence these last few days, he wondered how more tears could possibly exist.

He wanted to brush his lips across her cheek but dared not with the reverend and banker nearby. So he only rubbed a thumb across her knuckles as he relinquished his hold and moved off.

Reverend Jones stepped closer to Mary, along with Mr. Hammond. Did they have things to discuss? Should he linger and support Mary? Perhaps that, too, was not his place.

Tearing himself away from the scene, he moved toward town. He would have to make a decision soon. Would he go crawling back to Pa and the ranch? Or seek employment elsewhere? But where? Still, today was likely not the day to pursue it. He wanted to be available for Mary.

Numbly, he walked in the direction of the boarding house, knowing his money would run out before too long. Still, it was a place for him to be right now, a place he wouldn't have to face his father...or his future. At least not today.

As he passed the General Store and the box of newspapers, the headline caught his attention. It read: THE PROMISED LAND IN OKLAHOMA!

What could that mean? Much of Oklahoma Territory had been left vacant after the War Between the States. Would they let just anyone claim it?

Intrigued, he fished out a coin he didn't truly have to spare and purchased the paper. It was rather farfetched—the very idea of it and the prospect that he might partake. But still, there may be a chance. Maybe, just maybe, this could be his ticket out of here.

CHAPTER 14

Anger

Mary sat in a chair watching Ma sleep. Sunlight filtered into the dim room through a thin curtain, but it did nothing to lighten Mary's mood. She did not know whether to be thankful or angry. Such was her situation of late. Ma improved. Her own ankle improved. But Pa was gone. And it in no way evened out.

Not that God kept score. Hadn't He given much? Forgiven much? Yet she could not deny that a part of her heart had filled with a strong ire. But if she were to be honest, was all of that directed at God? Or was there more than enough for herself?

Thoughts of what she could have done differently, *should* have done differently...or said...plagued her. Yes, Pa knew she loved him. Yes, Pa had gone to a better place. But that didn't mean she had to be well with it, did it?

Reverend Jones had been thoughtful and kind. But she had stomached about all she could about God's provision and plan for her. She believed it was true. Still, that didn't change her feelings on the matter.

Ma shifted in her sleep.

Mary leaned forward to catch a glimpse of her features. Was she waking? It seemed not. Ma's eyes were closed and her breathing deep.

The silence did not serve Mary's mood—it only intensified her agitation. Leaving someone alone with their thoughts was one of the worst things in the world. Especially in grief.

A light knock on the door frame drew her attention. *Thank goodness...someone to talk to!*

Dr. Shaffer poked his head in the room. "How is she?"

Mary tried not to let her disappointment show. "About the same—resting."

He nodded. "Good. That's the best thing for her."

Mary looked at her mother's form. Ma had pulled through the worst of it. There was, then, reason to be glad.

"You have a visitor." Dr. Shaffer's voice surprised her.

"A visitor?" As if she didn't know who it would be. David had promised to come by today. Their exchange the day of the funeral had been brief. It almost seemed as if he feared she would break at the wrong word. Must he think her so fragile?

"David Matthews." Dr. Shaffer's tone was rather gruff. Did he disapprove? Did it matter? "I told him to wait downstairs."

She nodded and rose. "Thank you." If the doctor was going to be curt, so could she.

He disappeared from view, but as she came to the doorway, she spotted his back as he moved toward the stairs.

Perhaps her sour attitude for the doctor had more to do with the piece of her anger that he owned. That part of her that wondered if he could have done more.

She sighed. It was for naught. Nothing he could say, confess, or affirm would change the result. Pa was gone.

Sucking in a breath, she thought on what she would say to David. Perhaps that would abate more tears. She had worn thin with crying.

In a few short moments, she had taken on the steps and the lower level to find herself at the clinic's front door. With as much bravery as she could muster, she opened it to find David, his back to her as he watched the townsfolk milling about.

He was strong—and not just physically. The way he had helped her in those first few days warmed her heart. Was it enough to thaw the frozen thing it had become?

She started to shuffle forward but paused. Was David here to tell her of his forthcoming departure? It was certainly long in coming. He had made no promises to her of staying or of a future. Indeed, she wondered why he had not already left. Hadn't he been due at his new route earlier in the week?

She drew in a ragged breath.

He turned, gaze taking her in, his features softening.

Goodness, how she admired him. Had always admired him.

He stepped to her and reached out an open hand. And waited.

It was only a couple of breaths before she slid her fingers into his waiting palm.

His thumb secured his hold on her and tugged slightly. "Let's get you off your ankle." He then urged her toward a seat just outside the clinic.

She offered him a smile she didn't truly feel but let him pull her and settle her on the bench.

He studied her face. What did he seek? His dark eyes provided a place of solace, such that she could not turn away. There was so little warmth left to her in the world, and she would not reject it when offered.

"How are you?" His words were barely a whisper.

What kind of question was that? Did he want the truth? Or should she tell him she was managing well enough?

"I...am doing all right."

He quirked a brow.

"As well as can be expected, I suppose."

His lips turned downward as if he doubted she spoke true.

"I'm finding my footing still." There, that was honest enough.

He rubbed her palm.

It caused pleasant tingles to run up her arm. Perhaps she wasn't totally numb after all. Still, she shouldn't get her hopes up. What had David come to say?

She decided to turn the conversation back to him. "And you?"

His eyes widened. "I am well enough."

She pursed her lips and looked down at their clasped hands, hoping to memorize the moment for what it was—her hand in his, her heart reaching for him. But something in her balked against it. The memories would only haunt her after he left.

"When do you leave for the stage?" There was no sense in beating about the bush. She steeled herself for his response.

"I, ah..." He licked his lips and peered down. "I won't be working with the stagecoach anymore."

"Oh?" She tried to meet his gaze, but he seemed to avoid it.

Until he didn't. Then he watched her. Was he waiting for more?

She cleared her throat. "Why not? I thought it was your dream to travel. To get out of here." The last word was choked out. She wished she could hide her nervousness better.

"It was...well, is. But not with the stage." He met her gaze, his eyes both piercing and tender.

What could he mean? "Did something happen?"

He sighed. "It's not important. I—"

"Not important?" She couldn't believe this. He had so wanted it. "Just tell me."

He glanced at the closed clinic door as if he expected to be rescued by the doctor's appearance. It was for naught. "They would not let me delay for the funeral, so I am no longer working for them."

He had given it up for her? That cracked the ice about her insides. He truly cared. But she didn't want him to give up his dream for her. "I didn't mean for you to do that."

"I know." He smiled and reached out to trace the curve of her cheek. It was the first sign of lightness in so long. "It was *my* choice. And I'd do it again."

She didn't know quite what to think. He had given it up for her. What exactly did that mean? There was no room to make an assumption, not from where she saw things. "What will you do?"

He straightened his shoulders. "I didn't come here to talk about me. I wanted to know how *you* were. How is your mother?"

She held up a hand. "Ma is fine, better even. But that's not what's weighing on me."

He stared at her. Did he understand? She couldn't make an overture but wanted desperately to know where she fit into his future plans.

"The stage would not have been right for me. For *us*."

Her breath shook. Was he saying?

"And I don't regret that decision."

She let her lips tip upward. This was some light in her darkness.

"But it doesn't mean I don't have plans."

Her heart swelled. "Will you go back to Stoneybrook Ranch?"

"No." His brow furrowed. "I...no."

That surprised, but she held off her dismay. He had a plan, after all—a plan that obviously included her.

"I read about this opportunity...in the Oklahoma Territory. There's all this land and anyone who wants a piece can have it. And I intend to get *mine*."

David watched as Mary's face fell. Drastically. What was the matter? Didn't she hear him? He wanted to make a place for them in Oklahoma. Their own land. Their dreams made reality.

"Your land?" Her words were strained.

"Yes...well, our land."

She swallowed. But her eyebrows lifted. Were his words hitting the mark?

"Our land?" There was a wistfulness to her tone. As if she caught the dream.

"Yes!" His hands moved up her arms. He wanted to pull her close, but he dared not. It was best to keep some respectable distance between their bodies.

"Our future..." Her tone was light and breathless. She *did* understand.

"Yes, a place for us to raise a family." He beamed.

Then her gaze drifted and the line of her mouth dropped. "But..."

He waited for her to continue, but she didn't. "But nothing. We'll have each other, we'll have our opportunity...our chance."

She met his gaze again. Her eyes glistened with unshed tears.

He had said something wrong, he just knew it. What was it? "Mary, I...may have misspoken."

"No," she said as she shook her head. "No, everything you said is wonderful."

"Then why the tears?"

She sniffled. "I just...I can't go with you."

And all of his hopes shattered. She couldn't mean that. "What?"

She refused to look at him, glancing down at her hands, now clasped in her lap.

He shifted his hold on her to capture her hands once more. "Of course we can. I'll be with you. We'll get married and set out on our adventure." He couldn't comprehend her reservation.

"You don't understand. I can't...leave my mother."

And his nicely constructed plan crumbled around him. But he grasped for the pieces as they fell. "But she's better. We can take her with us. Maybe I can secure our land and send for you and your Ma."

She shook her head, gaze still set on her hands. "I can't do that to her."

"What do you mean? What grandmother wouldn't want to help raise youngins? And I'll make sure to build a place for her. You'll see." Even to his ears, it sounded as if he reached without thought.

Mary's eyes caught his. "I wish that were true. But her condition...she wouldn't survive the trip. And can't be so far from a doctor."

He grimaced. These things had not occurred to him. "But..."

"I just...can't lose her too." Tears streamed down Mary's face.

And it broke his heart. "Surely we can figure something out."

She stood rather abruptly. "I'm sorry, David. I won't do that to her."

He rose, reaching for her again as he insisted, "I promise, we'll figure something out."

"I need to check on Ma." She pushed past him and rushed

as much as she could into the clinic, slamming the door behind herself.

He took a couple of steps in that direction, preparing what he would say when he caught up to her. But he halted. There was nothing. Nothing he could think of that might assuage her fears or answer her concerns.

An anchor filled his gut.

He moved off in the direction of the livery. He'd been in town too long. It was time he got out of here to think, to gain perspective, to...just go.

It took short work to secure a horse for a couple of hours. Mounting, he looked in the direction of the clinic.

And pushed the horse to go opposite.

Wisdom

David scanned the area in front of him. How had he ended up here? And just what did he hope to gain? For there was no longer solace for him at this place...only tension and strain.

But as he stared at the overhead sign swinging in the wind, he studied the weathered letters that made up STONEY-BROOK RANCH. It was home...but it wasn't. Would it always be this way?

His gaze settled on the cabin across the pasture. Maybe this was why he had come—Ma. She always gave sound advice, but more than that, she listened well. Always had. Yes, that was his reason for being here. Not some secret desire to torture himself by creating more challenges and heartache.

Putting heels to the horse's flank, he steered the animal down the dirt path and toward the cabin. He attempted to keep his gaze centered on his destination. No good would come from seeing Pa at the barn or in one of the side paddocks. It would be best altogether if Pa didn't know he had come.

Slowing the horse to a halt, he dismounted and secured the reins to a post. He paused briefly. The smells of the ranch—the horses, dirt, even Ma's flowers that surrounded the porch—always put him at ease. He hadn't realized just how much he was giving up when he left.

But he couldn't let that deter him from his mission. He refocused on the cabin and climbed the few steps onto the porch. Then he knocked on the door.

No answer.

He knocked again, louder.

No answer.

Where was Ma? Might she be in the back of the house? He thought about pushing in, but it wasn't *his* home anymore. It wouldn't be right.

Perhaps she worked on the laundry around the side of the structure. Still, she should have seen—or heard—him coming, wouldn't she have?

Either way, he saw no harm in stepping across the front of the homestead and looking around the corner. He wanted to shoot a glance toward the barn, but again, he decided against it. What good could come of that?

Peering to the side of the home, he spotted fresh laundry on the line, but still no Ma.

That wasn't cause for worry, though. There were many reasons she might be unaware of his presence. Even after his being here for some minutes.

He turned, but not quick enough to miss Pa's approaching figure.

The man looked up at the same time. And their gazes clashed.

David had an urge to shake free of the stare that now pinned him. It fairly consumed him. But he would not. Not with Pa watching him.

Pa halted mid-step.

Should David back down? Speak a quick excuse and race for the horse?

"David?" Pa's deep voice pulled at him. It was not accusing, rather he seemed curious. Pa shifted his stance. "What are you doing here?"

"I came to see Ma." David had neither the desire nor the inclination to lie.

"Ah." Pa picked up step again, moving toward the porch. "She went to check on Mrs. Jones. She's been stuck at home for a spell."

"I see." David glanced at the wooden boards beneath his feet. What was there to say? If he needed an excuse he'd best come up with one quickly. It wouldn't be long before Pa stood on the same porch. Facing him. Saying who knew what?

But he was at a complete loss. And remained so until, indeed, Pa got to the top of the stairs.

"Is there something I can do for you?" Pa's words were solid, but devoid of emotion.

David supposed he deserved as much, letting the tension between them brew as he had. "No. Thanks." He stepped forward, bypassing Pa and moving toward his rented horse.

Then he stopped. What made him stop, he wasn't certain.

"You could wait here. I expect her back in the next thirty minutes or so."

David turned slightly and glanced at Pa. The man's voice may be wiped of emotion, but his features were not. A glimmer of hope shone from eyes rimmed with lines of weariness. And his mouth curved down on one side, betraying more than a hint of sadness.

Dare David think they might overcome their differences? Make peace? Perhaps that was farfetched. But he could aspire to heal the rift.

He surprised himself and said, "Sure." The word came out more confident than he'd expected.

"You want some water? Or coffee?"

It was a fine offer. One he should take him up on if he wanted to mend what was broken between them.

He nodded.

"Here, sit a piece and I'll get a pot started." Pa indicated one of the chairs beside the front door. "Unless you'd like to come in?"

"No." David was quick to say, then amended, "It's a nice day. I'll sit out here."

Pa gave a quick nod and stepped into the house.

David pulled in a shaky breath as he sat. What was he doing? How was he to go about this? Once again, he wished he knew better how to pray. For he lacked divine intervention to open the way for him.

He gazed at the flowers, fresh in bloom, waving in the wind. And he remembered what had brought him this far. His thoughts felt heavy as he considered Mary's words. And the manner in which she had said them. Was there any possible future for them? One where he could follow his dream and still have her in his life? If not...could he sacrifice one without tearing in two?

Pa returned with steaming mugs. He handed one to David on his way to the other chair.

Though the brew was sure to be hot, David sipped a bit. It about scalded his tongue. Pa always did like his coffee especially heated.

They sat in an uncomfortable silence for some moments.

"I, ah, heard you aren't with the stagecoach anymore."

David forced himself to keep his gaze on the dark liquid. How could Pa know that? He hadn't really told anyone. Was Pa keeping tabs on him? Either way, there was no sense in denying it. "Yeah."

"Any reason you decided to stay?" Pa was fishing. But at least they were talking, so David let it go.

"I am not staying." He wanted to offer more, but felt stilted by the tension.

"Oh. I see." Pa took a swig of his coffee. "Where you headed next?"

The question was quieter than David anticipated. As if his father struggled just as much as he in this exchange.

"Oklahoma. For the land rush." Why was he only speaking what details were absolutely necessary? He prodded his own tongue. "But..." What was he thinking? How was he to finish that sentence?

Pa watched him. David could feel the man's gaze.

David let out a long breath. "I am at a crossroads." He finally glanced at Pa.

The man muttered, "A crossroads? How so?"

"I have—ah—approached Mary Foster. I want her to be a part of that future."

Pa nodded. "And she won't go?"

David shook his head and, leaning forward with elbows on his knees, examined an ant moving across the porch. "She says she can't—with her Ma ailing."

Pa released a burst of air as if he had held it in for too long. "David, I need to tell you something. Something I should have said years ago. And more so...a month ago."

David turned to look at him.

"I judged you too harshly."

What?

"I had hopes of you taking over the ranch. And it bothered me you didn't want that too."

That was an understatement.

"My own Pa had plans for me. Wanted me to take over his farm."

David tried to keep his features in check. And wasn't sure he succeeded.

"But I had a dream for myself. A hope for my future."

David bit at his lip. Why had he never heard Pa speak about it this way?

"And I took it...with my Pa's support." The man sounded solemn. "And in the years to come, I worked hard to make this life for me and your Ma. But there were times, especially when my Pa died, that I wondered if I had done right."

David's brows came together.

Pa looked down again and pressed out another breath. "I never saw him again. Oh, we had letters, but I never looked in his eyes again. See, I didn't take into account what my leaving would do to them—my parents, my brother and sister. It took a toll on them, too."

David thought about his words with Katie the day he left. Had he hurt her? It had been clear Ma was uncertain even as she supported him. Pa's concern and worry was more apparent now. It wasn't only about rejecting his birthright, Pa didn't want David to make a rash mistake. One that he'd have to live with for years to come.

"True, I want you here, but I see now that it's not about me."

David's eyebrows shot up. That was quite the admission. "I know that, Pa. Now."

"So, I'm sorry for being stubborn. And for trying to hold you back. I only want what's best for you."

David swallowed. And realized a lump had filled his throat. "Thanks, Pa."

"But I also want you to know that I never could have done this without your Ma. I fell in love with her and God blessed me with her love in return. That has been the biggest adventure of my life. None of this," he said as he waved about himself as if to encompass the whole property, "would even matter if she weren't by my side. None of it."

David sat straighter and examined his own heart. What would it be like to take a chance on Cripple Creek? For Mary. To abandon his hope for more and find hope right here? The grand adventure on the stage had not been what he had hoped...maybe the plan for Oklahoma never would have satisfied him either. Maybe nothing out there would. Maybe it was more about finding peace within himself. With Mary. How much had he let her in? How much had he held her at arm's length? And what would happen if he truly opened his heart to her?

Mary watched the scenery around her move past. Dr. Shaffer had been kind enough to see her and Ma home. But what would home be like...without Pa? Would it feel empty? Solemn? Lonely? For certain, it wouldn't be right.

Now that Ma had come around to herself more, she had not handled the realization of Pa's death well. In a word, it crushed her. And she had been quieter of late. So much so that Dr. Shaffer had feared a relapse. But in the end, both he and Mary saw it for what it was—grief.

As difficult as her own grieving had been, supporting Ma in her pain and still managing her own weighed on Mary. How was anyone supposed to do this?

And Mary was doubly sorrowful at David's rejection. That day, the last time they spoke...she had watched from the clinic window as he walked to the livery and took off. She had not seen him since. Not that she expected she would.

Still, she would have liked to talk to him once more. If nothing else than to apologize for her behavior and bid him farewell. She did wish him well on his next adventure. And was glad she wouldn't be holding him back.

She sighed and looked behind herself to where Ma was reclined in the bed of the wagon. It was time she focused on her mother and helping her get better and more stable. This daydreaming would not serve either of them. Least of all her.

It was high time she learned that. And move on.

CHAPTER 16

Discovered

David walked out of the telegraph office, a frown on his face. He had expected better news. Staring at the black ink on the telegram wore on him anew. Even after groveling, the stage company opted to pass on his offer. That would have helped him earn a solid living and still be able to see Mary from time to time. But it was not to be.

Now what?

He wanted to go to Mary and tell her everything. But he needed to offer her something sure. And that was something he didn't feel. How was he to support her? To keep her and her Ma comfortable without steady work?

Glancing across the street to the clinic, he pondered what his next course of action might be.

After his talk with Pa, the way was open for him to return to the ranch. Yet that still didn't feel right. Maybe it never would. And he hadn't the chance—or desire—to explore that. Why did he avoid it? That may be a question for another time.

He looked up and walked toward the General Store. Perhaps there was some work that Mr. Yerby had heard about. Even if he had to work as a farm hand, he would.

As he neared, he spotted someone in his periphery. Turning to look more closely, he noted that it was Jonas. And he headed straight for David.

Must he? David wasn't ready to face the man and admit he had done naught with the opening Jonas left to Mary's hand and heart.

"Hello there!" Jonas stretched his legs and waved.

David couldn't politely ignore him any longer. So he paused and waved back. "Hello to you, Mr. Anderson."

"Please...Jonas." The man let out an exasperated grunt. "How are you on this fine day?"

"I've been better." David fairly grumbled. Why did he tell Jonas that?

"Oh? Why so glum?" Jonas indicated that they should continue on their way.

David picked up step. "Things didn't work out with the stagecoach. Or with that run on land in Oklahoma...at least not for me."

"So you've decided to stay?" There was a level of excitement in the man's eyes.

"I had. But work is not easy to come by."

Jonas chewed on his lip. "Maybe you're just not looking in the right place."

David's eyebrows gathered. "I'm all ears."

"Well, I happen to know that they need more men at the mines."

David chuckled and shook his head. "I'm sure they do."

"Say what you want, but it's good work and decent pay." Jonas scoffed a bit. Had David offended him?

What Jonas said was true enough. But David had always heard horror stories about cave ins and the mine conditions. It was not something he wanted to be a part of. Much less seek out.

"Never mind." Jonas waved a hand. "Forget I said anything."

"No," David said on a sigh. "I should apologize. It is honest work. I just never thought much about it. How has it been for you?"

"It's not a glamorous job, that's for sure. But it's something a man can be proud of. And the work's not difficult on the one hand. Not too much brain effort. But it can be rough in other ways." Jonas laid a hand on his arm and circled that shoulder in its socket. Was it sore?

"I suppose so." David considered Jonas. What would it be like to take on that kind of job? Sure it wasn't highly considered, but it was respectable.

And...it would give him a way to make money and stay in Cripple Creek. The reasons he had summarily dismissed the idea before became vague in that moment.

It wasn't quite the adventure he had wanted, but maybe that wasn't what his heart truly craved. Perhaps it was more about Mary. Besides, maybe in a few years, he could find different work. Or he and Mary might be free to strike out on their own. The future was wide open. If he could find something steady for now.

And just for now, this could be it.

Mary tucked Ma in for bed. The woman had not spoken two words together since coming home. But Mary was grateful that Ma's strength returned. Even in some small measure. It gave Mary confidence that Ma had years left to her life.

She made short work of cleaning the kitchen. Two bowls, two spoons, and a pot—how difficult was that? But she might as well get used to it. There would only be the two of them to clean up after for who knew how long. She certainly didn't.

Maybe she wasn't meant to marry. Maybe she had always been intended to be on her own. That was easier to tell herself than to embrace the sting of losing David. It was too much.

There would come a day when Ma was placed to rest with Pa. Then what was an older maiden to do? Ma's sister and her kin were a stage and train ride away. Would that be Mary's future? The spinster cousin?

Wiping her hands on a towel, she looked about the cabin that now felt too big. And, as she suspected, far too empty. No jovial Pa with his warm baritone spouting off figures and telling jokes. He had always kept them laughing over something. Now, all was silent.

Mary moved to the front window and watched as the sun began its descent over the horizon. The sky would burst into a myriad of colors soon enough. Perhaps she could find some measure of joy in that.

At the end of this day, she knew in her bones that God was with her. She struggled to think Him good, but in her heart, she trusted that He was. That may be the only thing keeping her level headed...and her heart bound up and healing.

Yes, she would be just fine as long as she had her faith. And no one could wrest that away from her.

A gentle knock at the door elicited a small cry from Mary. So deep in thought, it had surprised her. With a hand over her chest, the rapid thud of her heartbeat assuring her she was still alive, she turned toward the sound.

And all was quiet. Had she imagined it?

Knock, knock, knock.

Someone was there. But who? Dr. Shaffer come to check on her before heading home? That was doubtful, but the most likely candidate.

There would be no solving the mystery until she opened the door.

As she approached the thick wooden barrier, she thought

better of it. Might it be someone wishing to take advantage? Wishing her and Ma harm?

"Who is it?" Her voice was shaky despite the weight she put behind it.

"David Matthews," came the muffled reply.

David? What could he want? Was he coming to wish her farewell? Could she be strong enough to let him and then watch him walk away?

"It's late, Mr. Matthews. Can we speak tomorrow?" She bit her lip to keep it from quivering.

"Please, Mary." His heartfelt plea was her undoing. "I need to see you."

Reaching out a shaky hand, she unlatched the door and let it swing open.

And there he was....tall, steady, and handsome as ever. Was it her imagination or was he, too, heaving?

"Mary," he breathed, and stepped within, close enough to touch her, though he kept his hands to himself.

The flood of emotions coursing through her had her wishing she might do just that...reach out to him. And the fact that they were alone came into sharp awareness. "Maybe we should speak outside."

She moved around him to the porch.

He followed, but she kept her back to him. He didn't need to see her feelings laid bare in her eyes.

"Mary, I found a way for us to be together."

She dropped her head. *He didn't...*

It just wouldn't do. She couldn't bear for him to give up everything he had planned and dreamed for.

"I...decided to stay."

She spun on him. "David, I appreciate what you're trying to do, but you can't. You can't yoke yourself to me when there is so much out there for you."

"That's not how it is at all—"

"But it is," she argued. And felt moisture pooling in her eyes. As much as she wanted him to think her stronger, she did nothing to stop the tears from falling.

"Mary..." Her name on his lips was heaven. "Listen to me." He settled his hands on her arms. "It's my choice. And I choose you."

She turned her head to the side, unable to fight him when his eyes held such adoration for her. It was everything she'd ever wanted. But it felt hollow if he would live to resent her.

He craned his neck to catch her gaze. "Believe me."

She shifted back toward him but directed her gaze to the space between them. "I can't let you."

"I already have. And not for you. For *us*." His words sounded so confident, so sure. She wanted to believe it.

She peered up at him. "You did what?"

He pushed out a breath. "I secured a job with the mines."

She pushed back from him. "The mines?"

He nodded, letting her step out of his grasp. "It's honest work. And it will allow me to stay here, to support you, and to marry you."

Her thoughts whirled. "What about your father? The ranch?" If he had to stay, there was better work for him, certainly.

He frowned. "My Pa and I came to terms with each other, but I can't work for him."

What did that mean? Why couldn't he work for his Pa? "I don't understand."

"I just..." David's gaze wandered then settled on her again. "Truth is, I'm not needed there. Pa is able to manage it on his own. And I need to be useful, to matter."

"But you do. Your family loves you. And they need you."

He frowned. "Not really. Pa is a self-made man. He's always managed on his own. And he will continue to."

She swallowed. "But you had such great plans. A grand dream of adventure."

He clasped her hands and drew in a deep breath. "I still do. But I was wrong. The grand adventure is not out there." He waved a hand between them. "It's here."

Her pulse raced. Could this really be how he felt?

"Mary, it's you. You're my dream and my greatest adventure. Whether we are here in Cripple Creek or chasing the hope of something more out there, I don't want to do life without you."

Tears now rolled. "Truly?"

"Truly." He tugged her closer and lowered his head, pressing his lips to hers. At first, a brush, a tender, soft movement. But then his arms came around her and held her securely as his kiss deepened.

She had never known anything like it. The sheer pleasure of the contact. And the rightness of the fact that it was David kissing her.

When he pulled back, he pressed a couple of quick kisses to the side of her face.

"Will you marry me?" His voice was low and yet gentle, wanting, seeking her heart as fully as he exposed his.

"Yes, David. For all my life before and to come, yes!"

In his embrace, and in him, she found that they were taking the first steps to the rest of their life. Together.

To find out more about David and Mary, pick up the first book in the Cripple Creek Series - keep reading for a preview!

Thank you, dear reader, for for reading along with me!

If you enjoyed this story, I would sincerely appreciate if you would submit a review. It would mean so much to me!

To read more about these characters, follow along with the Cripple Creek Series. Find it at:
https://saraturnquist.com/cripple-creek-series/

The stagecoach moved along, bumping and rocking as it went. Trees and other green scenery whisked by the window. Views of mountains and open plains were visible from the seat of the coach, vistas familiar to its occupant. Katherine Matthews was coming home. She returned to Cripple Creek, no longer the scared, unsure teenager who had left to further her education so many years ago with hopes and dreams of a new life in a new place. No, she had matured into a confident young woman who had grown in stature and in beauty. Her hair was no longer the mousy color she always hated, for it had deepened into the same beautiful chestnut brown she had always admired in her mother's appearance. She'd grown out of her awkward teenage features, and was now well regarded among her peers as a rather handsome woman.

Returning to Cripple Creek brought many rather-mixed emotions to the surface. Imagine, one of her first postings would be at the same schoolhouse where she received her educational start. When her mother wrote to her of the interim need, she was glad to help out. What an odd coincidence that the letter would find her, too, in transition. Would this turn into a permanent placement? Did she want it to?

The mountain scenery became more recognizable, and she thought back on her childhood. There were so many happy times here. Unbidden, her mind wandered to the day of the great tragedy that had marred her spirit—the day Ellie Mae died.

Even all these years later, she carried the scar in her heart. The events of that day had left her broken. Why must thoughts of Ellie Mae plague her so? And all the more as her return became imminent? She shivered as the images from her nightmares the previous evening flitted across her mind. They would not stop. These same visions visited her in sleep night after night. All the more frequently these last weeks.

Closing her eyes, the hazy images took form and became memory. It was as if no time had passed. She and Ellie, walking through the schoolyard just as they did every other day . . .

Hooking arms with Ellie Mae, Katherine stepped out of the schoolhouse and into the yard. A rather large group of students gathered off to the right near the old tree. It didn't bother Katherine. She turned her attention toward the path that would lead home.

"What do you think they're up to?" Ellie Mae whispered.

Katherine glanced in that direction and noticed Betsy Callaway at the center, flapping her jaws. Why would anyone listen to anything she said? But they did. The class at large seemed to adore Betsy. It didn't make sense. Clenching her teeth, Katherine grabbed for Ellie Mae's hand. "Whatever it is, we don't want to be involved." She pulled Ellie Mae along as she walked on, trying to pass the gathering.

"I know Miss Matthews couldn't do it," Betsy said loudly.

Katherine froze in her tracks. What had she just said?

The crowd of students parted and glared at Katherine and Ellie Mae.

"Let's keep going," Ellie Mae pleaded, tugging on Katherine's hand.

She should listen to Ellie Mae and not become a part of whatever game Betsy played. But she could not let Betsy get the best of her. What would everyone think of her?

So, she turned to face her accuser. There stood Betsy with Wyatt

Sullivan, the most popular boy in school, right beside her. Betsy's blonde pigtails, tied back with perfect pink ribbons, shone in the sun. Her dress was no less perfect, pink with just the right amount of lace and even a slight puff to the sleeves.

"Do what, pray tell?" Katherine shot back. Her heart beat furiously in her chest.

"Go down through the mine shaft." Betsy folded her arms in front of her chest and raised an eyebrow.

Katherine's heart skipped a beat then, but she tried not to show her fear.

Ellie Mae's grip tightened on her hand.

"I assure you, Miss Callaway, it's not that I can't do it. It's simply that I have better things to do than to be traipsing about a mine shaft." She turned to leave and hoped that would be enough to silence Betsy.

"Prove it." Betsy's voice rang out after her.

Katherine's eyes slid closed. Was there any way around this? "I have nothing to prove to you," she called back over her shoulder.

"Fraidycat!" Betsy laughed.

The other students joined in.

Katherine's face burned. A fire had been lit within her. She was not afraid of anything! Releasing Ellie Mae's hand, she then whirled around. "I am not afraid!"

"There's only one way we'll believe that." Betsy's hands moved from her chest to her hips.

There was no way this would be a one-way challenge. "Are you going?" Katherine poked her chin out, putting her own hands on her hips, attempting to puff up her chest as much as she could.

"Of course," Betsy said, though her voice caught.

"Then, let's go." Katherine grabbed after Ellie Mae's hand and headed out in the direction of the old mine shaft. She hoped Ellie Mae didn't feel how her palms had started to sweat. Perspiration covered her whole body. How was she to keep up this façade?

The group of students followed, a din of voices behind. As they neared the cavernous opening, they became quiet as they halted several feet short of the forbidden place.

Wyatt pushed through the crowd once they had stopped. "Now, girls, this is foolishness. Talking about it is one thing, but you're not actually going down there, are you?"

Katherine glanced at the mine opening. It looked dark and ominous. Not what she wanted to see. Then she eyed Betsy. She had everything— the popularity, the most handsome boy in school ... But she would not have Katherine's pride, too. "I am."

"Then I am, too." Betsy stared at Katherine, matching her glare through slitted eyes.

"Kath-rine," Ellie whispered, tugging on her hand.

Katherine looked over at her friend. Ellie's eyes begged her not to go. Katherine wondered again at the danger. Her friend had every right to be concerned, she supposed. But it would not last. Betsy would go but a few steps in and give up. Katherine was sure of it. So, she would not be dissuaded.

Wyatt's eyes moved from one girl to the other. A couple of years older than the girls at their thirteen years, he stood a good head taller than Katherine. At last, he threw his hands up in the air. "Then I'm going too."

"And so am I," came Ellie Mae's quiet response.

Katherine leaned toward her friend. "Ellie, you don't have to go." Her eyes held Ellie's. What was she going to do? She couldn't take Ellie into that place. But something had eased in her when Ellie Mae volunteered to go. Was it selfish of her to want her friend to accompany her?

"Yes, I do." Her voice was firm, though her chin quivered. "I'm sticking with you."

A bump in the trail jolted Katherine from her reverie. The scenery outside became blurred. Or was it her? Touching her face, she felt moisture. She wiped at the tears. This would not do! Whatever happened when she returned, Katherine was determined she would face it with as much bravery as she could muster.

To read more, find *Hope in Cripple Creek* on my website:

https://saraturnquist.com/hope-in-cripple-creek/

Faith in Cripple Creek (Book 3)

Jane Millington has come to Cripple Creek to visit her friend. But a few bumps along the way land her face to face with a man who would rather not become entangled. Not that Jane is looking for a relationship.

Saddened to find her friend struggling after the birth of her child, can Jane offer the hope that she needs?

Timothy Johnson still lives with the sting of betrayal. And he is determined to never risk his heart again. But a chance encounter with a woman who is only passing through leaves him curious.

Can Jane and Timothy offer healing the other so desperately needs? Will they be able to see beyond past hurts, lean into faith, and find love?

Love in Cripple Creek (Book 4)

A woman burned by love. A man who has lost his way.

Betsy Callaway hasn't been the most upstanding person in Cripple Creek...and she has now passed the acceptable age for marriage. But something about her calls to Nikolai "Nick" Hammond's heart and draws him back home.

The antics that ensue between the pair and the obstacles they face--including their own stubbornness and becoming entangled in a bank robbery-- threaten to keep them on separate paths, but their draw to each other pushes them together.

Will the prodigal find home welcoming? Can Betsy hope for real redemption?

And the prequels...

Lauren Crawford is nothing she should be. Put off by the War between the States and her own experience on her father's plantation, she longs for something more. Under the control of her parents, there is not much room for anything but submission. Still, she dares to defy them...

The war changed Tom Matthews. And he has plans of going beyond his father's humble farm. He will do whatever it takes to make those dreams come true. Until he finds himself drawn to a southern belle he would rather despise. He is soon caught up in a situation not of his own making.

How much is too much for the one he loves?
Dare he sacrifice his dream?

In the rugged terrains of Cripple Creek, David Matthews' world has always been overshadowed by his father. Each sunrise over Stoneybrook Ranch reminds him of the path laid out before him—a life scripted by expectations he isn't sure he can live up to.

Mary Foster has held a silent affection for David since their youth. And while her mother suffers the ravages of a disease they fight to contain, Mary's heart patiently beats in the hope that when David finds his place in the world, there might be room in it for her.

Will their paths diverge in the vast expanse of the frontier?
Or perhaps love can guide them to find in each other the very thing they are lacking in themselves—home.

Acknowledgments

This is truly one of the more difficult things to write...to narrow down who to thank. Because there are so many people who contribute to my work and who make this possible.

Cindy Smith and Kelly Hollman, thank you for reading my work as it comes together and helping me see the places it could be stronger.

For my Novel Academy Huddle, your prayers and ongoing support are priceless.

VerBull Photography, I continue to love the headshots and your gift for capturing my "good side."

Julie Sherwood, thank you for your efforts and expertise... my work is so much better because of you!

Becky Brabham, your talents make my words shine!

Cora Graphics, time and again, you give my books a great "face" through your cover art.

My family, thank you for loving me and supporting me tirelessly. Even through deadlines.

My readers, you keep me going.

Sara is a coffee lovin', word slinging, Historical Romance author whose super power is converting caffeine into novels. She loves those odd little tidbits of history that are stranger than fiction. That's what inspires her. Well, that and a good love story.

But of all the love stories she knows, hers is her favorite. She lives happily with her own Prince Charming and their gaggle of minions. Three to be exact. They sure know how to distract a writer! But, alas, the stories must be written, even if it must happen in the wee hours of the morning.

Sara is an avid reader and enjoys reading and writing clean Historical Romance when she's not traveling.

Please follow along with her journey through her newsletter at: http://saraturnquist.com/list

Happy Reading!

facebook.com/AuthorSaraRTurnquist

instagram.com/sararturnquist

x.com/sararturnquist

youtube.com/@SaraRTurnquist

pinterest.com/sararturnquist

Also by
Sara R. Turnquist

CONVENIENT RISK SERIES

A Convenient Risk

An Inconvenient Christmas

A Less Convenient Path

A Convenient Escape

An Inconvenient Acquaintance

These Golden Years

A Less Convenient Arrangement

Ranch Hands Collection (ebook only)

LADY OF BOHEMIA SERIES

The Lady Bornekova

The Lady and the Hussites

The Lady and Her Champion

The Lady and Her Secret

RAILWAY ROMANCE SERIES

Laura, The Tycoon's Daughter

ACROSS THE YEARS SERIES

Among the Pages

Between the Lines

STANDALONE NOVELS

The General's Wife

Trail of Fears
Off to War

www.ingramcontent.com/pod-product-compliance
Lightning Source LLC
Chambersburg PA
CBHW021709190726
48289CB00008B/2452